a leaf in the whirlwind

Shivasharan D N

INDIA • SINGAPORE • MALAYSIA

ISBN

Paperback 979-8-89277-550-2
Hardcase 979-8-89415-231-8

FAMILY TREE

Shunka
Vaisaki (w)
Kubja Vengadi
Vengappa
Lacchu (w)
Raju
Asobha (w)
Vanka
Arobha (w)
Asobha
Raju (h)
Arobha
Vanka (h)
Atura
Rani (w)
Rupini
Chandra (h)
Rama
Venga
Aruna (w)
Aruna
Venga (h)
Aguna
Rathi (w)

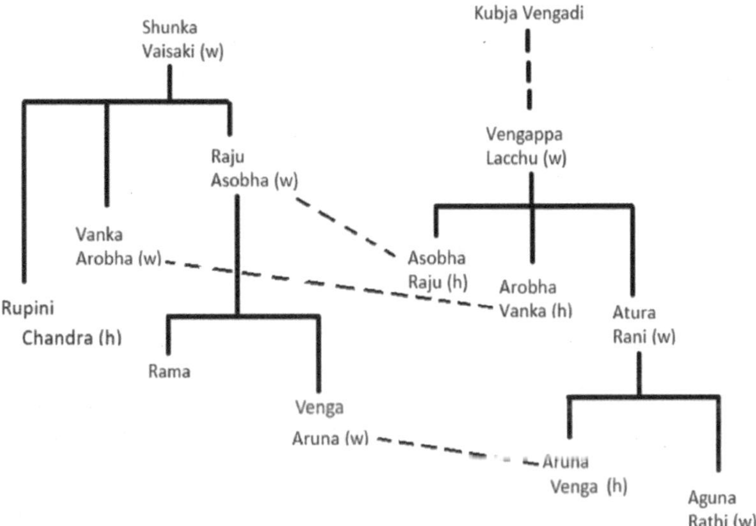

Dedicated to

my uncle

Abbani M. Narayanappa

Thanks to

my teacher

R. Suresh Babu (JNV Chikkamagalur)

Contents

1
The Path of the Dead

He had no idea it was going to be his last meal, that too an unsatisfying one. A small lump of ragi still lingered on his lips and the wild-spice chutney dripped from his protruding tongue's tip. The throat looked defeated before swallowing that last bite. The blurred eyes bled tears while his head shed pints of blood from what was the hardest blow this man had ever taken in his life. For a second, his mind struggled to fathom what had just happened. It was not that pain was new to him. It was just that he couldn't imagine, however briefly, why such a thing had to be inflicted on him, or anyone for that sake. Pain had always evaded his understanding of life, even after being on the receiving end of it for his whole life.

His mind started to give up before he could taste the sense of things around, though hardly a few in his life thought he had any sense, nevertheless. He felt pulled by some force. Before succumbing to the injury, the images stored somewhere from his grandmother's epics and fables ran like flashes in his head. Random words kept echoing while the strange sceneries from nowhere in his life fought with the familiar ones to live their last moments in his mind. All the tastes of his life came lingering out of his brain and were put back on his tongue, attempting to erase that fervorous monotony of the last bite of ragi-lump that he was tasting – along with the wild-spice chutney. The scent of the flowers; the aura of the temple shrines; the touch of the grassy mud at his feet; and the smell of his grandmother's dark room – slowly slumbered into finding a place in the oblivion. Before he could breathe his last, he slipped out the lingering bite and chanted, "Rama Rama!" For once and ever, the voice of his chant resonated with the devotion carried in his grandmother's utterance of Lord Rama. His tears were no more out of grief. He exhaled his last breath with a smile.

The world, with all its mighty beauty and amalgamated cruelty, disappeared from Rama in a snap. His eyes froze while his broken skull kept bleeding. The scene stood as a testament to the cruelty of the world and agitated the serenity of life around him. The sun hid beneath the dark clouds which carried no sign of rain. The trees rattled out of tune with the cacophony of the birds. Howling dogs roared while the cicadas mourned in silence. Nonetheless, no synergy could summon Rama back to life. He had been liberated from all the worldly disturbances... finally! He had never pondered death in his life. He had never pondered life either. He had stopped making sense of anything in life when he took a blow even before he could walk or talk. At the most, death happened to him just the way life happened, without being bothered by his thoughts.

Ranga was the first to notice Rama's body, lying orphaned in the tentacles of nature. The narrow embankment did not leave much room for his herd of sheep to walk. He noticed that the herd he was shepherding diverged slightly under the jamun tree. What he thought would be a boulder turned out to be a body stiffer than a boulder. After identifying it was Rama, he cried out for help. A man from the neighbouring village, Arali, who was loitering in his farm fields, came running from a furlong towards the cry he just heard. Minutes later, Venga arrived at the scene. Ranga uttered upon noticing the brother of the deceased, "He is not breathing." Venga haunched down and checked for the pulse as was already done by Ranga. Venga confirmed the loss of breath and the pulse. He looked up at the tree. Seeing the broken branch on the tree, he shrank his face and said, "My mother had warned him a thousand times not to play with trees. Finally, what she feared has happened." He sent out Ranga to bring the village nurse to the entrance of Bani. Later, he took the help of the neighbouring villager to lift and shift the body to the village entrance. Upon reaching the gate of the village on a motorbike, the nurse, who was already brought by Ranga, quickly performed a preliminary check and confirmed the death, her words shivering. However, as a safety clause, she said, "It is better if you take him to the hospital once." Upon hearing that, a villager behind the nurse shouted, "Take him to the doctor in Hutha, he is close, and he is reliable," which broke the ears as well as the ego of the nurse who was standing next to that villager. Several quips followed. "Let us call Muniya. His kashaya can wake up even the dead!" "Try to feed him water. Check the wound and try to stop it from bleeding." "He is not bleeding anymore," Ranga replied to the last bit of an ask. Byrappa erupted from the crowd, and looking at the body, shouted, "Hey, shut your mouth, all of you. Ley Venga, let us take him directly to Klar hospital." Without even waiting for Venga's response, he went to start his Tata Sumo. Venga followed him in silence. Even before the body was shifted into the Sumo, people in a lot rammed into the vehicle where the dead body could find a place only on the laps of toiled men. The Sumo which went to Klar returned to Bani in no time, bringing the same body and the same news – of death. Asobha, the mother of Rama and Venga, was outside her house, waiting in unison with some of the villagers. In the middle of the cacophony around the death of her son, Asobha was reminded of her younger days when she had lost her husband and was surrounded by the same milieu. The mother, who had her reasons for the lack of tears, veiled her mouth with the tip of her saree. Her face had sunken just enough to give the onlookers a hint of loss.

Asobha spent hardly any time crying for the next two days. She was barely seen outside her room. She wasn't exactly interested in participating in any rituals either. However, after the night of the third day, the tears rolled incessantly but with no sobbing. Every now and then, the people around her took note of her tears and attributed them to the usual grief of a bereaved mother. But, like every onlooker at a bereaved house, they could not contemplate the depth of her agony from her unmoving face. She spent every moment of the later days in the corner of the hall, where Rama's portrait was placed garlanded, slanted against the wall on a small stand. A tall and lone lamp shone fiercely in front of it, to burn away the darkness of death from the dampened lives visiting the place to offer their last prayers. Any attempts by Asobha's younger daughter-in-law, Aruna, to feed her a bite or a sip, went in vain. And some, especially the youngsters in the close family circle, started wondering how she sat fixated in the same place for days without ablutions. It was not until the eleventh day, for *thithi*, that she was displaced. It was done at the insistence of her sister, Arobha and a few others, who also lent their hands in dislocating her pungent body from the corner. She had to be dragged by Arobha and a couple of neighbours. Out of respect, Aruna evaded the dragging positions, took a place on the other half and held the legs along with the bottom edge of the saree, in an attempt to lift Asobha. While dragging, they couldn't ignore the weight of her loss as well as the stench of grief from her body. She was pulled off the corner like a dead deer from the hunt. Asobha barely noticed herself being dragged, bathed or dressed. When she was dropped at Rama's memorial to perform aarti to the tulsi and was handed over a bunch of incense sticks, she wept like a baby. The tears rolled while attempting to water the tulsi plant. Arobha moved in an attempt to console her, even though she knew it was futile. Ajjamma, an old lady from the village, asked Arobha to stay back and let Asobha vent her grief in full gush. When her husband, Raju had died, Asobha thought it was the dreariest moment, as – contrary to her wishes and prayers – her fear of dying as a widow had come true. And more importantly, thenceforth she had to take care of two children all alone. She had never thought she would witness her husband's death before hers, let alone her son's. But now that her son had died, there was remorse along with the grief. At the venue of any death, it was hard to remain oblivious to the fact of how soon the dead went missing in the presence of those who grieve. It was a testament beyond doubt, to the harsh reality – at the end of the day, only life matters to another life. All the attention, sympathy, care and help that the left-behind were offered; as if it was the left-behind who experienced death. The people gazed at the grieving mother with all their attention, sympathised with compassion and then walked towards her house for the *thithi* meals. Only Venga, her younger son, resisted looking at her – not even a peek. He maintained a little distance from her all the time.

ഈ✦ര

There seemed to be no time for him to weep. The last few days, Venga had immersed himself in getting all the rituals done right according to the customs. He wanted no one to raise a brow or point a finger at him or his family for any lapse. Relatives and villagers offered whatever help they could. However, by himself, he did not seek any. It seemed as if he wanted to do all the funeral work by himself. On the day of the cremation, he had made sure the cow dung and varieties of wood were arranged on time and in place, along with a load of ghee. He bought more than enough white clothes to wrap the body with, and enough perfumes to keep the body in fragrance until the last of the acquaintances had their final peek. He arranged for the drummers to call upon the village for the cremation. As they would do at any ceremony, the drummers came libated. To avoid the beats turning from grim to celebratory under the influence of libation, he even appointed an acquaintance to look after the drummers – so that the drums were struck in accord for the occasion, all along. He chose the people himself to carry the body on the chosen path along the village road, and the right elder to guide him in performing the requisite rituals near mid-path, and also during the cremation. As required by the custom, in the absence of a child or the father, as Rama's only sibling, he put all his efforts in an attempt to lead the dead towards *mukti* and set the pyre. The cow dung cake, covering the frozen eyes, slid away during the burning. While everyone was looking at the fuming pyre, Venga was captured by Rama's eyes. He could see his brother's eyes through the flames. He saw the discharge of tears from the burning eyes, being vaporised and dragged upward in a trice, disappearing into the sky. Slowly, the discharge started turning maroon. All he could see now was the maroon drops emanating from those eyes, and dissolving into flames. He was losing himself in the fire of burning eyes. That was when he felt the elder shaking his shoulder, and asking if he understood what was just said to him. He nodded with a no and asked him to repeat. The elder explained that the funeral pyre ritual was done, and he had to return to his home where the body had rested and light the lamp which was already in place. He also warned Venga to not look back, step back or stop for any reason. "Walk until the house in continuum and in silence, like the time is and like the time your brother no more has," the elder commanded with intent. As if it was just what he wanted, Venga left the place in one stride.

Even on the third day, during the ritual of milk-libation, though he kept himself occupied, he could not forget the sight of the maroon lines emanating from his brother's eyes on the pyre. The hairs which fell off Venga's head while shaving for the ceremony turned maroon. The water into which he dipped himself for the bath turned maroon. He could see only the maroon borderlines of the white loincloth that he wrapped around his lower body. Anytime he had to apply *kumkum,* he also had to suppress the tinge that was caused in his brain by the sheer colour of it. He fostered a new loath in himself to the colour maroon. Right about the time he had enough against that colour, on the day of *thithi*, his mother arrived at the memorial. The woman, who grieved in silence until then, started her incessant display of sorrow. Her tears too turned maroon to him, and he just hit the edge of his frenzy when she lamented, blaming herself for the death of Rama. He was about to snap at her when Byrappa and other elders unintentionally intervened, by walking near to him in order to convey their condolences and then, to take leave from the place. He hid his frenzy, bid goodbye to the elders, and went to a distance to calm himself. Arobha, who was serving food to all, noticed Venga sitting in isolation at a distance. She served a portion of all the dishes brought as offerings into a plantain leaf, slid it on to her palms one after the other, and tiptoed towards Venga lest food from leaf-full would be spilled. Leaning in front of him, she said soothingly, "Don't mind. None of your favourites are on the menu. I will cook something for you in the evening." Rama's favourite dishes were to be served as a ritual. Whatever the family assumed Rama's favourites could be, they were cooked and offered. Suggi lumps, beetroot palya, ragi-lump with *avarekalu saaru, khara* pongal, a tiny mound of rice with pepper rasam poured all over, cut portions of several fruits – including plantain, and a few more items made their presence on the leaf in marcels. Khara pongal was added to the menu at the insistence of Ajjamma from the village. Venga took a stark look at the leaf and shot it off Arobha's hands in full fury. "Don't bother, just go!" he shouted. The gathering at the distance turned their eyes in unison towards the sharp sound they just heard, like a herd of gazelles turning to the trumpet of an elephant elsewhere. While everyone stayed silent in bewilderment, Aruna rushed to the spot with concern for both her aunt and her husband. "What happened?" she asked Arobha. "I don't know. I just offered him food." Arobha replied with a hue of confusion on her face. "Please, don't mind. Go there and manage the *prasadam* for the crowd," Aruna said, pointing to the gathering and attempting to ward off Arobha's confusion.

As it had been the case all along their married life, calming Venga in the moments of frenzy was something only she could do, something that she enjoyed doing too. Venga had never contemplated as to why he turned meek in the arms of Aruna, but he always did so with ease. Aruna sat closely beside him. "What happened?" She spoke just two words but gently at his ear like the sound of a flute, clutching her right palm into his left and rubbing his forearm with her other palm. He turned his face to her. She seemed to be appealing with her eyes. His face started to melt. "What else should I do? You know how he was. He was born to denigrate my house. He never let us live in peace when alive. Now, my mother is shouting all these unwarranted words. What is the need to blame herself for his death? How can we protect someone who roams around the villages like a monkey and brings humiliation to the house? I have been through enough because of him. Now, my mother has started her own drama. Seems like no one cares for the people around!!" He said in a single breath. Aruna continued her consoling by rubbing his hand and said, "Whatever she says for the next few days, try to bear. She has just lost her son. Whatever he did when he was alive doesn't matter anymore. Don't try to find meaning in a bereaving mother's words. They will fade away in a few days. Let her vent everything out."

Brushing the tears coming out of his eyes Venga said, "We bore him for so long in one hand while trying to protect our family's honour from his deeds with another. If my father were alive, he would have killed him in his childhood itself for the things he did." Aruna thought he was a little harsh in choosing such words. However, she could feel his emotion, having come from the mighty Vengadi family. On the other side, near the memorial, Asobha was gasping breaths through the past and was blabbering, "You should have been alive! It was you he needed!" While the people around were wondering whom she was talking to, someone was tingling her through memories.

✦

Vaisaki got off the auto-rickshaw and entered the hospital looking for her son. He was supposed to be waiting for her near the gate. She had no familiarity with the hospital, its atmosphere or its crowded public. She hadn't even stepped inside the compound when she smelled the pungent scent of tincture, pills and wet beds. The sun was up above her head. She held her bent hip with her left palm and placed the right palm vertically against her temple, allowing the shade to comfort the eyes which were searching for Raju. She limped with effort towards the entrance. As she approached the hospital porch, her percolating sight caught a glimpse of his face. She started moving towards him. As she approached him, she was irked by the scene of her flirtatious son with a nurse. Raju paused his laugh abruptly at the sight of his mother which made the nurse turn back and check what horror was behind her. It was just an old lady. But when he addressed the old lady as '*amma*', the nurse fled the place. Raju took his mother to Asobha's wardroom. He left the mother-in-law and the daughter-in-law alone with an excuse to buy fruits for the ladies. As soon as he left the room, Vaisaki wasted no time. She started narrating what she saw on the porch and warned Asobha to keep her husband in check, lest he would fall trap to whimsical vagaries. She went on to say how, during the pregnancy of wives, the whores of the village and elsewhere become concubines; and how if remained careless, the husbands would escape the clutches of the wives towards a lost cause.

Asobha was not surprised when her mother-in-law ratted her son out. Vaisaki's anecdotes of how she had kept her husband, Shunka, in check, despite bearing three babies, were the basic knowledge inducted by the family and the neighbours into any new woman freshly acquainted with Shunka's family. Of course, the story was not void of myths that come with adulation. When they heard it for the first time, the two daughters-in-law, Asobha and her sister, Arobha, had been blown away by the way their mother-in-law saved the fidelity of her marriage, given the minute details with which it was told. The narration added the fervour to the story. Regardless of the narrator, the tale sounded astounding. It was as if every narrator had inherited the story, in words and spirit. And Vaisaki's daughter, who was the youngest of the three, was more than acquainted with the story by the time she got married. It had become her fantasy to relive figments of imagination from her mother's life – of controlling a man who is her husband, keeping him in check with the magic of her love, and carrying the sanctity of a three-knotted bond to eternity. However, Vaisaki never corroborated nor took credit for any part and parcel of her tales. Instead, she skirted the vicinity of the narration scene whenever she heard, or even got a hint of her cliché story. No one ever knew who started telling it for the first time, and after all those years, no one cared. The part of the tale, where it was narrated that Shunka made love with Vaisaki only five times from the day they consummated the marriage, until the last child was born, gave the most chills to the audience, and even sprung in them their highest sympathies for Shunka. The audience would all awe in consonance when someone would add that part of the story, which told that she even had two miscarriages between the three surviving children. Immediately, someone would, in jest, point out the possibility of having had sex only once for each pregnancy. And, another person would push the joke further by saying, "*I hope it was at least once for each pregnancy, else the story would lose its purpose,*" and that was when all would burst into laughter. And, that was when Asobha would usually intervene, and put a break to any distortions that would malign her mother-in-law. Thanks to Vaisaki's aloofness for her own story, she never overheard the satirical parts of it. But Asobha failed to contemplate why Vaisaki would brush away from being part of the conversations where her story would come up. She even remembered how her attempts to butter her up with adulations went in vain, whenever she tried to use the story as a setup. Nevertheless, Vaisaki's aloofness could not stop Asobha from being inspired by the tale in its pristine form.

Now at the hospital, having just gone through the most experiential event of her life, lying tired with a smile of achievement, Asobha listened for a while with calm and regard to her mother-in-law, although she was just complaining about her own son to her own daughter-in-law. But, the serenity of calm and regard started losing the place on her face when Vaisaki started telling some of the incidents happening on her back in the village, while she had been lying on the bed in the hospital. An ominous air struck her in the face, turning it blue. The thought of her marriage tale, taking a diversion from the chastity, tickled and tinged her nerves. Her body jolted with chills. Vaisaki was wary of warning her daughter-in-law in the presence of no one else, lest the news would spread far into the nooks and corners of the village. She also asked Asobha to keep it to herself. And she promised that she would aid Asobha in keeping the husband in check. And that the time to be ignorant or the time to take things for granted was over, with a son in the lap. The jolts, which struck Asobha, made her hardly hear anything that was said later. When she returned to a somewhat normal state, she realised that no one was there in the room. The baby was crying, and she had no idea for how long. The feeble voice in the cry had failed to wake his mother up from the turmoil she was in, nor did it have the strength to reach out of the four walls to call for outside help. The cradle was just beside her bed. Partly coming out of her shock and heeding the cry, she bent to her left in an attempt to pick him up, half-mindedly, forgetting the injury she had just borne from the surgery. She had no problem lifting the baby up. However, when she tilted back with the baby in her hands, the suture ripped and the pain hit her hard. It was so painstaking that she shivered and slipped the baby for a moment, and hit his head on the side rail of the bed. Coming back to sense instantly, with instinct, she held the baby from further fall.

She trembled, not in pain but with fear. She held the baby tightly to her chest, yet she could not stop it from shaking in her trembling hands. For a moment, she loathed herself. She slid the veil from the boy's face to take a peek. He was not crying. Not anymore. Instead, with eyes closed, he was smiling like he was having a blissful dream. She drew a respite from that smile. The sound of his head banging the rail resounded in her head, but louder. She unveiled the hood that was covering his head, repenting at the same time for not covering him in a thicker towel when Vaisaki had asked her to do so. "*That would have cushioned the blow,*" whispered a voice in her head. As she inspected the baby's head, she felt no bleeding. She moved her finger around the scalp of the guava-sized head to feel a bump, if any. Feeling no bump, she relieved herself from loathing. Her husband entered the room and asked what she was looking at. She tucked the hood back to his head and said she was just checking the baby. She hid that incident as clumsily as she could in her heart, and the boy hid it as a lump in his head. She spoke to no one about it, and the boy could never tell anyone. Raju looked at his son's face. The baby's smile, which was seen for the first time after two weeks of birth, excited him. "Look how beautifully our boy smiles," he cherished. The spouses exchanged smiles with pride and kissed each other. The baby kept smiling. Little did the parents know that that smile had rendered the anger of a wife waste, and it had pushed a husband out of imminent infidelity. She had forgiven her husband's flirtations in silence. And in her clemency, she hid her clumsy mistake of negligence.

Asobha had quelled her anger towards Raju, though it wasn't that easy. If not for her child's headbang and her involvement in it, she would have burnt Raju alive with her tantrums. She hailed from a family tree in which each branch had just enough food to feed a nuclear house for the last few generations. However, each one had pride and vanity enough to spread into the surrounding fifty villages. The Vengadi family was named after *Kubja* Vengadi, the first acknowledged ancestor. He was known to have donated thousands of acres of land to the poor and the needy who set up their families in and around his village, Katilu. His name was Vengadi, but due to his short physique, he was surnamed *'Kubja'*. After five generations, everyone in those fifty villages still thought that the proverb, "*Form is short, but the essence is vast*", took birth from the physique of Vengadi vis-a-vis his quality of generosity. Anyone from around who acted generously was adjectivised as *'Vengadi'*. However, the people within the Vengadi family saw both glory and gold only during his tenure. After him, the only thing left for the family to spread was people. The vastness of the Vengadi family had remained only in size, not in wealth. And, each nuclear family was separated and left with a meagre meadow and means to feed just one nucleus. Yet, they never gave up the pride they were associated with. Every one of them attempted with every breath to ooze out the family honour. Asobha and Arobha, as sisters, brought that pride with double vigour to Shunka's family when they married Shunka's sons, Raju and Vanka. Coming from such a revered family, it wasn't easy for Asobha to digest that her husband was pushing her away, looking for pleasures in the arms of other women. It was oceanic depression and volcanic anger that had clouded her that moment in the hospital. And it was from that state that she was pulled out by the smile of her baby, just after she banged its head to the rail.

❦✦❦

The Shunka family grandly welcomed her back from the hospital. They fed her whatever she desired and she did whatever she desired. No one antagonised a new mother who bestowed the family with a progeny. It was the duty of everyone else to make sure that they acquainted themselves with her whims and urges, and got accustomed to serving her well. Whatever service had been offered to her during pregnancy was offered with further fervour, and was extended to the baby too. Everyone in the family took up a chore and cozied the place for her. Especially the husband; he found a new zeal in serving the mother of his son, rather than his wife, for a change. He made himself scarce to the rest of the family and the village. Eventually, there was no more of him seen, flirting or otherwise, along with any other woman in the village. He attended to the farms, worked or oversaw the work, and returned home well before dusk. In the evening he engaged himself in taking care of the mother and the son. A couple of months passed. He had quelled all her doubts and served her a fresh love with his care. Asobha was growing happier and happier, and dreamier. In between sometimes, the knell of Vaisaki, about how the whores of the village turn into concubines during pregnancies, woke her from the dreaminess. Sometimes, she thought of inviting her husband back to her bed as soon as she could. She consulted her friends, who affirmed that the waiting period, for bedroom affairs after pregnancy, could be cut short. She had many means at her disposal. Upon realising that she had more edge than her mother-in-law had had in her times in terms of bedroom affairs, the knell of Vaisaki stopped beckoning her.

After a few months, Raju started caring less about managing the house affairs with an excuse to be with his son. Asobha started to replace him in all those matters. She took care of Vaisaki. She started offering her help to her sister and brother-in-law in their chores. She was the one whom Vaisakhi approached first with regard to any family affair. In fact, Vaisakhi grew fond of her more than she was of herself in dealing with the family, especially regarding keeping it together in one piece. But it wasn't long before Asobha's vigour was to be put to the test. Arobha, though married at the same time to the same family, had not borne any child. She tried to be happy that her sister delivered a progeny. But, she could hardly resist envying, with time. It was almost a year after Rama's birth. Arobha started rumbling her dissatisfaction with murmurs. It grew into cries of melancholy in a few months. All began with the kind of treatment Asobha got from the family for bearing the child. Every time Arobha paid heed to the special treatment her sister and her child got, she started breeding a desire for the same, slowly and silently. However, she could not conceive. Instead of a child, she incubated the desire. The desire grew for long enough to give birth to the resentment – the resentment she had gotten against the life of her own sister and the nascent life she had given birth to.

It was Vaisaki who delivered the 'baby boy' news to Arobha. The apparent reaction on her face was a smile. Later, with time, she surrendered the sibling-love to envy. Her envy and resentment started turning into tantrums with her husband, which emasculated Vanka. She kept screaming and blaming him for her misfortune of not becoming a mother. When she got married along with her sister, she was welcomed into the Shunka family just like her sister. She had entered into the alliance boastfully. She had found pride in the alliance with the fact that Vanka was well built, if not more handsome, than her brother-in-law. But then, as her life was swinging out of balance from that of her sister's, she yearned for that which her sister had. Vanka was hapless. It was not that he wasn't trying. He tried to console her with all his might but to no avail. One night, the tantrums fell out of their bedroom window and reached Vaisaki's ears. It pricked her to hear a sign of discontent between a husband and wife in her family. An incident from decades back churned her mind. She prayed to her deity Rama and came out of the sunken mood, as the next morning was the eleventh-month shower for the newborn progeny. Sullen minds wouldn't be auspicious to the house, and especially to the child, who was about to be washed for good. She gently walked by the window, warning the husband and wife, "Hey, what is that noise at this time of night? Wrap your bedsheets and go to sleep. We have a lot of work in the morning." The bedroom was silenced and the house went to sleep. The old lady went out and lay down on the veranda bench, wrapped herself in a woollen sheet, and slanted her support-stick against the wall on the head-side. The woollen threads in the sheet were pinching. Despite the discomfort, she fell asleep, looking for the morning.

Raju had woken up before the rooster-call. Without even heeding the morning ablutions, he went straight to his farm field to look after the load of potatoes which were to be taken to the market. Vanka, too, had woken up and been to the field to pump the water for the current crop during the early morning hour of single-phase electricity. Asobha woke up a little later and was out at the gate, sprinkling water. The cow dung to wash and cleanse the entrance floor was already kept at the gate in a *mankari*. She layered it on the mud floor and decorated the dung-coated floor with red and white rangoli flour. Arobha was busy with house chores. After washing the utensils and cleaning the vegetables, she started cooking the first meal of the day. The old lady, who had finished her morning ablutions, the bath, and the prayers, entered the kitchen asking for a sip of coffee. She was aware that that was where Arobha would be at that time of the day. She gently asked her what the fight was between the husband and wife on the previous night. Arobha did not reveal anything. She gave a reason which carried no truth and tickled no sense. '*Who doesn't hide their envy and pettiness under the veil?*' Vaisaki tried to brush away the previous night's event as an aberration. But, from then on, she kept a keen eye on both Vanka and Arobha.

By the time the sun shined on the entire village, Raju was back home with a load of mango leaves, chrysanthemums, jasmines, firecrackers, marigolds, few stem-cut plantains and a lot of stalk-cut plantain leaves, bunch of fresh bananas, guavas, a gunny bag full of shelly coconuts, neem branches, tulsi leaves – something of almost everything that was grown in the fields. He had made sure that he brought everything Vanka had asked him for the catering purpose, and also what was asked by his mother for the ceremonial rituals and aesthetics. Apart from those, he had also plucked anything he thought could be of use for the occasion. When he arrived home with a bullock-cart load of edibles and plant parts, everyone had their own opinions about the bountiful load. His mother knew he was what he was; his wife smiled at his excitement for their child's first-ever divine ceremony; his brother thought he always did extra work than what was expected of him; his sister-in-law thought he would go the extra mile as long as it is for his own blood; relatives thought he was more than excited because a '*son*' was born; and others thought he had resources in abundance to squander. All he did was to immerse himself, jubilantly, in the celebration of life that had come, safe and sound, out of his marriage. He lit up the place and served everyone around with his liveliness. He had plucked and pulled all the stuff which was dear to him in his life, with no regard for their necessity and wanting. The load of ecstasy was apparent in his run of the day.

The festivities poured into the house as hundreds of relatives, and tonnes of village folk kept visiting the house throughout the day. The vibrance was so high that by the night, everyone had lost all their energy, including Raju, who usually behaved like a walking stone. Nonetheless, everyone was happily tired. Afterall, the best thing to toil for and lose strength was in celebration. The celebrations went on for a few more months and then took a grave pause. The father failed to live long enough to hear his boy call him *'appa'*. The boy lost his father before he could keep him in his memories. How-so-ever, the father was to exude in the coming days, in the exuberance of the boy's life.

2
A Grave Turn

Rama grew up to be known for his smile, from his neighbourhood to the village to the school. Not sure if it was his father's exuberance or the fatal blow he had taken in the hospital that made him smile all the time. Wherever he went and whatever he did, he always had a smile to spare. When injured, he smiled. When praised, he smiled. When scolded, he smiled. When loved, he smiled. When spited, he smiled. Until the age of eight, the smile of that child looked enchanting and adorable to any soul. The situations at which he smiled were water under the bridge. No one had ever judged the smile or the face bearing it – at least, not until he graced with a smile, at what was supposed to be a disgraceful deed, and his face failed to wear that shame of disgrace appropriately.

One afternoon, during the lunch break at the school, sitting under a neem tree, Rama was looking around the place through a piece of sun shade glass which he had just extracted from under the dust. Through the glass, he was noticing how the shade of light changed from place to place, tree to tree. But one thing that caught his mind was the coconut trees. The ferns of the coconut trees at a distance glittered and fluttered in colours, like that of the feathers of a peacock, while the rest of the trees showed no such change of hue. He didn't understand what was happening, but he could not hide his intrigue. He moved the piece of glass along with his site, investigating all the surrounding trees. Somehow, only the coconut trees looked special. '*Is it because the ferns of coconuts are thin and narrow commensurate to their branch size, just like each filament from a peacock's feather is commensurate to the entire feather?'* His contemplation was disturbed by a classmate, who came running to inform him that he was summoned into the staff room.

In the last five years, he had gotten used to visiting the staff room to receive acclaim – regarding his academic prowess and co-curricular achievements. Only this time, something else was waiting for him. A barely familiar adult male was sitting opposite the principal. Upon Rama's arrival, the science teacher, who stood beside the principal, signalled the strange person and said something to him which was inaudible to Rama, who was entering the room at a distance. Hearing her, he turned infuriated, stood up, treaded towards Rama and slapped him with an unwavering intent. Clueless and puzzled, Rama gazed at the man, rubbing his cheeks in an attempt to alleviate the pain. The man started throwing tantrums, "How dare you behave like this? Is this what your mom and dad have taught you? Scoundrel!" Rama asked the man, pleadingly, why he was beaten, but with the usual smile on his face. "You have the guts to ask 'why'? You don't know 'why'? You don't know what you did? Look at him smiling! Have you no shame?" He was infuriated further; he slapped the boy again and kicked him on the butt. The boy countered, but he did so without losing the smile on his face. The principal intervened and stopped the man from inflicting further assault on the boy. The smile on the boy's face, while he was thrashed for an allegedly humiliating cause, gave the principal an impression of him being smug. A smile on a face can have any meaning, and sometimes, no meaning. But, the predilections have a knack for getting carried away. At that moment, the smile on Rama's face made the principal lose the sympathy which he had felt for the boy just before he stopped the adult from beating him. The boy still stood clueless as to why he was beaten. He started to request the principal to call his mother, still smiling. The principal warned that if called his mother, she would beat him more than the strange man, and asked him if he knew who that man was. Rama nodded with a nay. He was told that was the father of Vaidhe, his classmate. Vaidhe had been nothing but a good friend to him. "*Why would the father of such a nice girl act like such a moron?*" He said to himself. He kept pondering the plausibilities while the principal discussed further actions with Vaidhe's father, Jana.

ꕥ✦ꕥ

Their friendship was younger and pristine than the womb of a gestating mother. They had met six months back after her Uncle Sukha had shifted to the west edge of the village, two-houses away and diagonally opposite to Rama's home. Vaidhe's mother, Suneena, was born in Rama's village and was married off to Jana, from the Maithalli village, situated three miles south of Bani.

In her childhood, Suneena's home in the village used to be a grand, beautiful, vintage house on the eastern edge. It was built by her grandfather. When the family split last year, they had to move to the western end of the village, where her younger brother, Sukha, built a small cosy home in the plot he had gotten during the split. Suneena and Sukha had lost their parents in their teenage years. The father got electrocuted near the farm field while jumping the electric wires to change the three-phase current to a single-phase. The mother, who was just a few metres away, heard a sound that felt like a bee humming close to her ear. After realising that it came from the transformer, she thudded to the spot and tried to pull him off. Both died on the spot. Thereafter, both the brother and sister were brought up by uncles and aunts, with a touch of love from their grandparents. They did not even protest when the property was divided during the split, though they were clearly discriminated against. They wanted to break on good terms with the rest of the family, with whatever came their way.

Suneena stayed at her brother's house whenever she visited Bani, although she met and wished well for the rest of her family tree. She had to circumambulate the village, at least once, every time she visited Bani, in order to spend some time with each of the split families. That's how big her family was and that's how dispersed they were. The village was full of relatives, but for Suneena, her brother alone reciprocated the love. Visiting him every now and then had become part and parcel of her life, especially after bearing a daughter and a son, Vaidhe and Varna. Jana was not very fond of staying away from his house. So, every time he visited Bani, he dropped his family off and returned to Maithalli in the blink of an eye.

Last summer, during Suneena's visit to Bani on Ugadi, she had been with her children and had celebrated the new-year day in grandeur. As usual, she had circumambulated the village, visiting all her relatives. And, when she had to return to Maithalli, Sukha had asked her to let his niece and nephew stay in Bani until Ramanavami. Vaidhe, who had been excited to stay back with her uncle, requested the mother to let her. As it was the summer holidays for the schools, Suneena could not offer much resistance. Vaidhe and Varna stayed back in Bani, and Suneena returned to her husband. The next ten days were to be a signature of grandeur in the life of Vaidhe. She would wake up early every morning, inhaling an auspicious breath and she would prepare herself to spend the day with her uncle. Every day, early in the morning, her uncle carried her on his shoulders with her tiny legs wrapped around his neck, like the snake on Shiva, giving her a heightened view of the world on their visit to the farm fields. When they hit the dried-up canal, he would approach close to the canal, hold her safely by her knees and lean her closely into the canal. She would scream in excitement, looking down at the depth of the canal from over his shoulder, as if it was an abyss. She would request him to take her away from the scary view. Sukha would move away from the canal laughing at her childish awe. On the muddy roads, she would attempt to reach low-hanging branches which she could not have reached herself, standing on the ground. At some places, he would pause for a few seconds to let her pluck a few tamarinds, guavas and in that season, the raw mangoes. She would pluck and eat a part of the fruit, and as soon as she found fresh fruits on the next tree, she would throw away the rest of the fruit in her hand, along with the seed. Sometimes, her uncle would point out to the saplings of some sort, in the canal and among the bushes, and he would tell her that they had sprouted out of the seeds, in the partly-eaten fruits, which she had thrown during her last visit. "*See, how all the fruits you threw away have grown into saplings. Whatever you throw, Mother Earth is giving life to it. You are not your mother's daughter, you are Mother Earth's daughter."* She would blush, he would poke her to chuckle, and then they would laugh out loud. She would ask him to get her down to take a closer look at the saplings. Touching the tender stalks and leaves, she would giggle in excitement at the sight and feel of them. Again, they would continue the procession. The parade of their walk and talk; her play with the cows and calves, sheep and lambs, at the farm, feeding and rearing them; playing in the water tank trying to catch the tadpoles; holding the small load of vegetables onto her head, freshly handpicked from the farm and carrying it to home; asking her uncle for chocolate from the shop when they reached the centre of the village, on their way back; this was the morning she yearned for. And, this yearning was what made her desire to spend holidays at her uncle's home. And, it was the same yearning for the pristine nature that brought her in touch with Rama.

Rama's house was diagonally opposite her uncle's house on the cul-de-sac, which ended with a big mound of sand, dropped for the purpose of building a house but had never been built. Beyond the mound was a private farm field where lima beans or ragi were usually grown. It was left barren otherwise. In the spring and summer, especially during the holidays, the kids and adults from the village turned it into their playground. The mound was the boundary for younger kids to play, beyond which they served either as spectators of the big games or as helpers to the big guys. Rama and his mates, for their age, stopped at the mound and played with their marbles, tamarind seeds or matchbox paper-cuts. Fewer girls preferred these games. Hence, if more of them were girls, they would prefer games like kabaddi, kho-kho, hop-and-chase or sand-dots challenge.

That day, Rama, Hari, Kencha and Varna were playing with tamarind seeds. Everyone chipped in ten seeds each and put them in a hand-drawn circle of around a one-foot radius. They took out their round hit-stones, which were a couple of inches wide. Everyone's hit-stone looked different as if unearthed from the unknown places of the village or elsewhere. Standing behind the circle, one by one, each threw their hit-stones close to the line, which was a few feet away from the circle. Whoever came close to the line without crossing it, got to play first. He or she would be followed by the next closest person. If the hit-stone crossed the line, they would fit into the precedence in the order closest to the line on the other side. Rama's hit-stone was made of granite, with a thoroughly polished circumference and the right amount of thickness to fly steadily in the air. Hari and Kencha also carried granite hit-stones. But, the thickness and the shapes were at odds for the game. Varna had one which was made of floor tile. He had gotten it from his uncle's home, where the bathroom was getting renovated and many broken tiles were laid waste. The stone looked fancy but lacked shape or thickness. Whenever he threw his hit-stone to get as close as possible to the line, the stone flew away and fell out of the line. The rest of them stayed within the line. And this time, it was Rama who took the first turn. Hari and Kencha's stones looked to be equidistant from the line. Varna drew a parallel line from Hari's stone and decided it was Hari's stone which was closer. Everyone remembered the order, collected their hit-stones and came back to the circle. Rama collected the tamarind seeds which were already placed in the circle and threw them from a little above the ground in order to spread them evenly around, within the confines of the circle. Two seeds crossed the boundary. Hari took one and Kencha took another, as they were next in the order. Hari placed the seed on the boundary line, and in one go, he pushed it with his finger to bring as many seeds, as close as possible. Kencha did the same with another seed. Rama looked a little disadvantaged. He had three avenues before to win the game, now there was only one. All the dispersed seeds on top of the circle, the vantage area, were spoiled now. He went to the line and noticed that there was a lone seed to his left side, but on top of it, there were other seeds in a lump. It was a difficult shot, but he took it anyway. As he threw the stone, it cut through the air and chopped that lone seed off the ground and out of the circle, and the stone bounced and flew over the other seeds without touching them. Rama had successfully chopped off a single seed out of the circle as per the rules. The kids, who had already lost all their seeds or who didn't know how to play, who had turned spectators, started shouting in excitement. A few girls, who were playing hop-and-chase, heard the noise and came running to be part of the euphoria. And Vaidhe was one among them.

The four players moved on to the next rounds. Kencha and Hari won a few rounds, but Rama was pocketing more seeds than anyone else. Varna was at a full loss. Most of the time, his hit-stone did not even touch the circle. It flew away from the circle like a chicken flying astray from a dog. Vaidhe did not like her brother Varna losing, but in temptation for the game, she enjoyed the euphoria around, as an onlooker, along with her friends. Varna checked his pocket, there were only nine more seeds left of him. The next round was played with nine seeds. Hari finished his turn as the first shooter and conceded. Kencha was at the line as the second player. On one side of the circle, a few feet away, Rama stood, waiting for his turn to collect the seeds. Opposite to him, across the circle, was Varna, praying that Kencha should not win and he should get his last chance to redeem a few seeds. As Kencha shot his hit-stone, Varna's prayer went unanswered. Kencha, with ease, chopped a seed off the ground and out of the circle, came to the circle and sat down to collect his prize seeds. Varna went pauper in front of an unusual crowd. He looked at his hit-stone; he was infuriated. In fury, he threw his stone away, with all his rage and might, in order to get rid of it forever. The stone, which had failed to hit the circle during the game as he intended, failed to fly away as he intended. Rushing through the air, the hit-stone took an immediate and sharp turn towards Rama, who was standing opposite Varna, counting his seeds for the next play. As if destined to be tactful, the stone missed the eyes and struck him in between them, at the top of his nose.

The nose started bleeding both inside and out. Rama felt his nostril bleeding maroon like it was spilling jam. In a moment, his feet and the ground around were soiled in his blood. The sight of dripping blood brought shivers in the kids who were witnessing the scene. Jolted, Varna stood dumbstruck. A girl in the crowd started screaming in fear and soon a few more followed suit. Hearing the hue and cry, a few more kids gathered around; one of them was Rama's brother, Venga. He started crying loudly on seeing his bleeding brother. While the crowd went bizarre, Rama stayed deaf silent, finding ways to stop his bleeding and holding his breath as long as possible to avoid the smell of his blood. On hearing the screams of the kids around, an old lady from a nearby house came running. She immediately held Rama's chin up, asked him to look at the sky, and told him not to lower his head unless asked to. She threw a few tantrums at the crowd, blaming their carelessness as a whole, and calling the game frivolous and Lunatic. The tantrums by themselves were not strange to the kids. But the blood was. Coming slowly out of the frenzy, the crowd started inquiring about the hitter. Varna, still shivering, stayed deaf silent. Hari, who was standing beside Varna just before the stone was thrown, shouted out the culprit to the crowd. The crowd, who knew that Varna had just lost all his seeds and mostly to Rama, started churning the revenge angle. The little mouths whined and showered their mighty vulgarity at Varna for throwing the stone, allegedly with intent. Venga whined and cried too.

Kencha, and a couple of others, had followed Rama to the old lady's house. She asked Kencha to bring a little cow dung from her backyard as she cleaned up his nose. The nose was not cut deep by the stone. She asked a lady in the house to bring the first aid box from inside. She cleaned up the wound again with tincture and applied a band-aid. She made him lie down on a wooden cot in the backyard. Kencha brought fresh cow dung. She handed it to Rama and asked him to smell it now and then. Rama was not allowed to get up until the internal bleeding stopped. When he woke up to go home, the old lady urged him to inform his parents about the incident and to visit a doctor. Rama nodded hesitantly and left the place. Enroute to his house, his friends, following him in a herd, urged him to complain to his parents about Varna so that he could exact revenge for the injury. Varna walked behind the herd in guilt. Vaidhe accompanied her brother. As the group passed by Sukha's house, Varna quickly slid into the house and disappeared. Rama's friends, who caught Varna escaping into his uncle's house, started murmuring. "Look how cunning Varna is! He escaped the moment he got a chance! Hey, Rama, don't spare that guy! Complain to your uncle. He will make sure Varna gets his share of pain!" said one guy. Another guy turned around to warn Vaidhe, who was still standing at the gate of her uncle's house. "Go and tell your brother. By tonight, he will be done. You haven't witnessed Uncle Vanka's fury."

Vaidhe rushed into the house and directly into their room to find Varna sitting in a corner with his head bent and sobbing. He raised his head hearing Vaidhe's anklets. She sat beside him and informed him about what she just heard from the boys outside the gate. He was even more terrified after this and cried like a frightened chicken. She asked him how he could injure someone for some disposable tamarind seeds. Varna explained the accident from his point of view. With redundant guilt and repeated words, he had never babbled so much in his life. She felt pity for him. But she couldn't avoid taking note of the irony. Varna wanted to abandon the stone which put him to loss and humiliation. Instead, the stone had abandoned him in style. The thought of the stone's mischief brought a laugh in her, but she suppressed it, being mindful of her brother's plight. She tried to console him as she hoped that among all that cacophony, Rama would have somehow recognised her brother's innocence.

The night passed without any anticipated dread. In the morning, Vaidhe woke up and started her journey with her uncle, as usual, and Varna slept till breakfast, as usual. In the evening, Varna did not go near the mound. He stayed inside the house and watched television. In the evening, Upon Rama's arrival at the mound, his close friends surrounded him to investigate the wound and sat down with him under the Indian Beech tree on which they usually played Monkey-chase. The bandage was still on the nose. Everyone fired questions inquiring about his state, his uncle's reaction and whether he complained about Varna or not. He answered them one by one. And when he said no to complaining about Varna, everyone was surprised. Kencha, his best friend, was disappointed and even felt betrayed. Kencha asked back in rage as to why he failed to complain, and how he could let Varna escape after what he did to him. Rama brushed it off, calling the incident an honest mistake. "Also, I did not feel any pain. So, why punish someone when there is no suffering?" Vaidhe, eavesdropping from a distance, heard his words. She was relieved that her prayer was heard and her brother was about to be vindicated for his innocent mistake. It was at that same time that she felt Rama's smile. On that bandaged face was that smile. She rewinded the day before's incident in her mind and took a look at Rama's face again. The blood-covered lips and chin were now decorated with that smile. His eyes had kept the same charm the day before. There was no surprise on his face, no tears acknowledging the pain. All she could remember hearing was his brother's cry and a few girls' screams. And, all she remembered about Rama was his serene silence.

Like she was pulled by something, she approached him. Standing in front of the boys, she called him by his name. Before she could say anything else, Kencha commented. "Look who is here. Ravana's sister, Shurpanaki." Vaidhe threw an angry look at him. "Ey, Kencha, I have no business with you. I am here to talk to Rama. Shut your mouth and sit. If you can't keep calm, find your way home. I won't spare your dignity if you speak ill of me or my brother again." It was enough of a dose to silence Kencha as well as his other friend, Suri, from bullying her any further. She explained to Rama about the day before from Varna's vantage point. After hearing the story, Rama replied to Vaidhe that he was glad she told him that. Before she dispersed, she informed that she was about to join his school in the fall, as her current school taught only until third grade, and that she was going to stay in her uncle's house for four more years until she reached high school. Rama asked her to get into section 'A' as that is where the rank students are placed, and she asked him back which section he was in. He said, "Section A". She smiled and ran towards the house, hopping on alternating legs.

✦

It was that first memory of her that Rama recollected as he moved from the principal's office to his classroom. The forty feet walk invoked more of such memories. Many hop-and-chase games he had played with her later that summer; several guavas, mangoes, jamuns that she shared with him, plucked fresh from her uncle's fields on her morning walks; a number of assignments he had completed on her behalf in the last six months; the moment when she kissed him and ran away while sitting together in the seemingly empty function hall, by-hearting a poem for the midterm exams. All along, she was nothing but adorable. He hadn't found such a dear classmate, and a friend, in the past three years. The more he recalled, the more difficult it became for him to seek logic in why Vaidhe's father treated him the way he did.

As he entered the classroom in silence, he looked for Vaidhe but in vain. He sat at his seat in silence. The school bell rang and signalled for the next period. The science teacher entered the class room, and the students stood up in respect for her. The first thing she did was to notice Rama. She was irritated by the smile on his face. She couldn't stop herself from ranting and humiliating him in front of the class. She went on explaining to the class how he still kept smiling despite the beating he had just gotten for his deed. She also asked him to quit the first row and sit in the last row from then on. He wanted to ask again, 'why am I being punished?' He was afraid that the same question would again draw more fury as it did with Vaidhe's father. Rama could only wonder at her tantrums as he moved to the last row. When he joined the school in first grade, the same teacher had asked him to take the first seat in the first row in appreciation towards his prowess in naming the animals and the birds. Everyone had been awed by his perceived knowledge then; for him, it was just another place to sit but closer to the black board. Now, he was pushed to the back row. Again, for him, it was just another place to sit, but a little away from the black board. The other students murmured their judgements without knowing the what-and-why of him, as the teacher left no stone unturned in naming and shaming Rama in front of the class. Before leaving for the day, the science teacher summoned him to the staff room again.

"Bring your father tomorrow!" she ordered.

"My father isn't there, Ma'am."

"Where has he gone?"

"He is dead."

"Oh! Okay. Then, bring your mother," she suggested. As he nodded and walked out, he couldn't avoid overhearing his teacher complaining to others in the room, "If one loses the father at a young age, this is what happens. The boys are bound to grow carefree and shameless. And, we have to deal with their nonsense." He couldn't grasp the depth of it. But he couldn't stop himself from pondering over it too. He exited, tiptoeing on his little feet.

It was not a normal day for him, even while playing with his friends after school. Most of them were looking at him differently. Some were appreciating him teasingly for becoming a big boy so early and started calling him early-bird. He was sure they were sarcastic, but not sure why. Some were teasing him about his genitals. It was as if everyone knew what he had done, except himself. When Kencha and Suri came to the field, he got the gist of everything. The rumours which had been spreading from the morning, why Vaidhe's father assaulted him, what the teacher meant when she shamed him, and so on. But, he couldn't shout back to everyone from that day that the rumour was not true. He hadn't kissed Vaidhe. In fact, it was she who had kissed him. He narrated his story to Kencha and Suri. Who else would believe him? Kencha asked him not to bring out the incident to Uncle Vanka, lest he would beat the hell out of him. Rama was never afraid of his uncle or his mother, though he had taken his share of beatings from them before. Also, after knowing the cause, he was not worried anymore. And as he knew what was happening, "*when the time comes, I can explain my side and vindicate myself. As simple as that*," he thought and relaxed.

The next morning, he took his mother to the school. A drama ensued in the principal's chamber. Until then, Asobha was not sure why she was called. As soon as the science teacher explained why she was brought in, Asobha became fierce and started slapping Rama in and out. And, on top of it, she accused him of not revealing such a perverse reason before bringing her to the school. "Why did you hide it from me? Should I hear the shaming deeds from others?" More rhetoric came out of the beating mother. His answers found no heed as the body took the beatings. The science teacher wasted no time in pointing to her mother about how he was not crying even the day before. "He has no remorse!" she shouted. Her words provoked Asobha to offer her beatings even more severely. The mother tried to bring out a few tears in her son's eyes to ward off the teacher. But she forgot to remind herself the last time she saw him cry.

Asobha dragged him all along the road until they reached the house, and she threw him at his grandmother. It was unusual for Vaisaki. She had never seen Asobha treat her son so severely. She asked which demon had gotten into her to behave that way. "Ask him what he has done. For pampering a fatherless child, this is how he repays!?" Asobha shouted in response. "What is this repaying and pampering and all? As a mother, you don't need a child to be fatherless to pamper. And also, this is a family, not a business. In a family, no one owes anything to each other as repayment. Shut your anger and tell me what happened," Vaisaki retorted. Asobha went on narrating what she heard from the teachers in the school, and how Rama behaved unapologetic, guilt-free and on top of it, kept a smile on his face, instead of tears, with no shame. "Looks to me from your story that no one heeded what the kid had to say," Vaisaki inferred. "What is there to heed? He has made a mistake and he is denying it out of fear. Why will a girl allege that she was kissed by some boy, that too at this age?" she asked, still angry. "Well, I am not sure if the boy would have grown any different if his father was here today. As I know my son, I can tell, he sure wouldn't have let others suppress his son's voice at least." Vaisaki said the final words and took Rama to her room, caressed him, gave him a handmade tamarind-candy, and let him sleep on her lap narrating a story. Before Rama went dwelling into his sleep, the grandmother's words muddled with his teacher's words and played the pondering game in his head. 'Would my life be any different with a living father? Vaidhe's father was there because he thought I wronged her. He was there protecting his daughter. Perhaps, my father would have protected me today, had he been here...' The thoughts kept staggering as he fell into sleep. The grandmother stopped her lullaby upon noticing him deep asleep. She rolled him onto the mat, cushioned his head with a pillow, and went out on a walk towards his son's grave.

3
MURMURS OF LIFE

Asobha recalled the incident from Rama's school when he was eight. Sitting next to his portrait, looking into the flame from the lamp, which was going to be turned off on that day, she judged the way she had treated her son. She introspected the way she had behaved. She introspected the way he could have felt. In the guise of honour and vanity, she had restricted herself from a lot of possibilities in life and had turned a blind eye to the innocence of her son. She had favoured the hypocrites and often, she had been the hypocrite. Only if she had tried to weigh her ignorance against a pinch of truth, could she have avoided what she did to her son in front of a bunch of unrelated people present in that august room. She started to wonder how she reached such an addiction to honour in life, over life itself. She recalled her mother's words first, from her childhood. "*Protect our honour, even if it takes you to lose your life.*" The words, meant in the context of protecting herself from the harsh realities of the world, had been morphed into having a different effect later in her life. She recalled how the stories of her clan's great ancestor, Kubja Vengadi, had always danced and dangled in her mind. And then, she recalled how she had ascended as the decision-maker of Shunka's clan, earning respect from her mother-in-law through her persistent discipline. She realised how, after Vaisaki's demise, she had de-facto held the bastion as the honour-keeper of the family, and how her sense of right or wrong took precedence in the family. She realised how she had secretly built an image of her own perceived house of pride and honour while growing up, which she would never let go for anything in the world. With the image she had built within herself, she had never been surer of anything in life. And now, sitting in a corner, aged and fragile, she had turned as unsure as she could about everything. The words of Vaisaki, from several years ago from her dying bed, resounded. "*Honour is like a garland that others wrap around our neck in appreciation. We should acknowledge and remove it as soon as possible. Never wear it like a necklace, and be conceited, lest one day it would turn into a noose.*" Asobha had brushed away those words, coming from a dying lady, as the rubble from a drying river. Now the rubble had turned into pearls, bringing out their value in the form of tears in her eyes, and guilt in her mind. If only she had heeded to the right words at the right time.

Arobha had stopped her attempts to console her sister after a day or two. Last eight days, she could only bear witness to Asobha's apathy in silence. Venga had taken himself the task of distributing the Eleventh-Day ritual cards, to all the required populace, and had kept himself busy in the last week. Most of the people he had invited were at his house on that day because of his mother, whom they honoured. But the embodiment of honour laid waste in humiliation in a corner of the house. Venga turned to treating all the guests well. He took his uncle's help in managing the catering, laying out *shamiyana*, and arranging tables and chairs in the backyard for serving *thithi* meals. His aunt and wife took charge of treating the Brahmins and the elderly guests for their needs and serving them with snacks and beverages. He hadn't spoken to his mother in a week. She hadn't either.

The gathering fulfilled all the customs. Thanks to the customs which weren't entirely pinned on one person. Every person was to be involved, especially the mother of the deceased. However, she couldn't do her part without help. She had to be supported by a couple of people on both sides to locomote, even within the house. A person had to sit beside her and help her lift a thing or two when the *mukti pooja* was offered, or hand over a thing or two into her numb hands. The entire day, her face was number than her hands. After the *pooja*, she asked her sister to take her to the bedroom.

Arobha requested her to eat something, to which she resisted. She was snuck into her room and tucked into her bed. The sleep, which the sloppy body had been yearning for the past eleven days, took her deep into a dream.

ꕥ✦ꕥ

Asobha was holding baby Rama in her lap and caressing him. Vaisaki was feeding cereal to the baby. Raju was sitting on the wall bench just beside Asobha, revering the scene. In a few seconds, without telling where he was going, he left the place and walked towards the graveyard of the village. Asobha woke up in a hurry to ask him where he was headed. In haste, she forgot the baby boy in her lap and dropped him to the ground. Vaisaki kept feeding the baby on the floor as the boy kept smiling, lying on the ground. Asobha went out of the compound gate and called out for her husband, "Reee... Reeee... Where are you going?" he did not turn back. "When will you be back?" He did not turn back. "Tell me when you will be back. By that time, I will cook your favourite coconut-holige." Again, he did not turn back. Returning to the compound in disappointment, she saw something lying on the ground and her mother-in-law was attending to it. She called for Venga, and he arrived with his moustache, wearing a *lungi*. Asobha asked him to clean the thing lying on the ground. He went in and brought a bag, filled it with the lump, along with the towel it was wrapped in, and started to move towards the garbage. The grandmother followed him with the bowl of cereal. "Hey, Venga. Wait for just a second. I will feed him one last bite. Please!" Venga did not heed his grandmother. She followed him till the street, outside the compound and fainted. After a few more steps, Venga met his Uncle Vanka. He inquired what was in the bag. Venga answered that it was some waste that his mother asked him to throw into the garbage. His uncle took the bag, looked into it, turned around, took note of people around on the street and said, "Why are you wasting such good dog food? We should feed it to the street dogs. We should treat them like family too." The crowd was clapping at the perceived generosity of Vanka. Venga smiled, took the lump out of the bag, along with the towel it was wrapped in, and placed it on a rock near the garbage, calling out for the street dogs, "tchu tchu... kreyy kreyy kreyy kreyy..." A few dogs came running from nearby, gathered near the lump that was covered in the towel, smelled it thoroughly and started feeding on it. Meanwhile, inside the house, Asobha suddenly remembered her little baby Rama, and she started looking for him. She came out and saw her mother-in-law who had just crawled inside the compound and was gasping for breath. Asobha asked her if she had seen Rama. Vaisaki, unable to speak, pointed her fingers towards the dogs. Asobha looked at the dogs and the towel that they were licking. She recalled that it was the same towel which she had used earlier to keep her baby warm. She realised what had happened. She ran towards the towel and chased the dogs away. Venga stood in bewilderment. She opened the towel and nothing was there. The towel was already emptied. She grabbed the towel and started crying slowly. Noticing that her hands were soiled in blood, she dropped the towel, turned her face up and away from her hands, and garnering all her might, cried into the sky, "Raa... Maaaa...!!!!"

✦

Asobha woke up screaming Rama's name. Hearing the scream that shook the house, Arobha came running into the bedroom. Venga, Vanka and a few other guests followed. After calming her down, the crowd dispersed with murmurs; the murmurs which were to kindle the public into tagging her insane in the times to come. The sister stayed back to console the barren lady. Venga went to the tent to manage the meal service. Vanka followed suit. Both of them made sure that every guest was addressed categorically and were served food to satiation. Bhadrappa and Byrappa, the elders of the village, were having their round of meals. Venga went to them, inquired about their wellbeing and also about the quality of the food. Both of them complimented the entire menu, and Byrappa told him how Bhadrappa had an extra *vada* as it was his favourite. Heeding to that, Venga looked around and called upon the person serving *vadas*. Bhadrappa resisted, Venga insisted. A couple more *vadas* were served onto his plantain leaf. Byrappa inquired Venga about his wife, "Where is Aruna? I did not see her anywhere." "She must be inside the house, helping my mother," Venga replied. "I heard that she is into her third month?" Byrappa asked. Venga smiled and said yes. Byrappa continued, "God's grace! He took one life away and is offering another. It's all part of his play." Venga's face paled out, but he exerted a smile at the irony pointed out by the elder. "Take good care of her. Feed her well. Always stay close and stay alert to her needs. You will have a wonderful baby born. May God bless you and your family." Byrappa finished his words. Venga thanked the elder with a *namaskar*. "I did not see Rama's wife anywhere. Where is she?" Byrappa asked. Venga shrugged in discontent. Bhadrappa intervened with a lower-than-usual voice, "Whatever the reason, it does not shine well on the one who misses the husband's death rituals." Venga replied with sarcasm, "It is not her first time with a dead husband. Maybe she is used to it." "Leave it. You never know what is running in her mind," Byrappa tried to brush the talk, by when Bhadrappa was done with his vadas. "All the items are so good. If Rama was here, he would have had a feast," Bhadrappa said to Venga, rubbing his stomach. "Most of the items cooked today were his favourites," Venga informed him. Byrappa took notice of Venga's concern for his brother and appreciated him. But Bhadrappa wouldn't stay quiet. "Rama had no favourites when it came to food! Whenever he visited my house, he ate whatever was served to him. He would sit on the floor with washed hands and crossed legs. He would always start with a quick prayer, and then, engulf in one go. Whether you offered him a *kaccha* mango or a plate of *biryani*, he ate with the same hunger and the same fervour." Listening to Bhadrappa's words, Venga turned humiliated with a hint of resentment for the words he just heard. Venga was infuriated to be reminded of his brother's nomadic nature, by which he went house to house in the village, wherever he was offered food, and ate without shame. For Venga, it was one of his brother's things that irked him the most as, in his perception, that was throwing the honour of his house onto the streets of the village. Byrappa noticed that Venga was offended by Bhadrappa's words. He also knew Bhadrappa would keep speaking out of mind and with no regard for the situation, when in the company of good food. "Hey, Bhadra, why speak of the dead now? Venga, you go and attend to your work. We shall meet after finishing the meals." Byrappa tried to brush away that awkward moment. Venga forced a smile out of his resenting face and went into the house in an attempt to get away from there.

He entered his room and rammed the door behind him. Aruna took notice of the discomfort by observing the way he entered the room. She went into the room to attend to him. Venting out his discomfort, Venga blabbered at Aruna about how Rama's deeds were still haunting him and his family, how his brother had cast an undying shadow onto his house. She consoled him, "Please, do not think of a dead man and his deeds. Let the dead be dead." "It is not that easy!" he replied. "But it is necessary. For your sake and our sake," she inferred. They spoke for a few more minutes and she asked him to draw some strength as he was the sole heir left in the family, and there were a lot of things to be done yet, and a lot of family affairs to be taken care of. It reminded him of that night's programme. He had already paid the advance and had arranged a stage drama for the night. A lot of preparation work was needed – setting the stage in the open field at the end of the cul-de-sac, setting up mics and speakers for the stage drama, setting up a small tent for the stage actors to dress and apply makeup, arranging the electric connection from the nearby transformer, et al. He took leave from his wife, asked his Uncle Vanka to manage affairs at the house, and headed towards the nearby town on his bike.

Before dusk, the stage was set and all the preparations were done with. The actors were to arrive and start the show. The drama was based on a portion from Ramayana's *Ayodhya-kanda* where Lord Rama was asked to go on exile into the forest for fourteen years at the behest of his stepmother, *Kaike*. Kaike was promised a boon by her husband a while back, which she had kept in reserve and chose to execute on the day before Rama's throning. She uses her boon to get rid of Rama, paving the way for Bharata, her own blood, to sit on the throne. The drama company had named the performance

"The promise of Dasharatha". The drama actors came at the sunset during the twilight. They took their time to finish their customary rituals before even talking about performing the drama. Everyone showered, dressed up in ceremonial clothes, and together, lit a lamp and offered prayers to Vinayaka, the remover of obstacles. They asked him to keep the evening, through the night, obstacle-free. They also prayed to Lord Rama whose story they were going to depict on the stage. After the *pooja*, Venga requested the performers to have food before they could begin performing. They refused in kind and asked for a glass of lemonade each, if he could offer. He served their interest, and after that, they went into the tent to dress up in costume. The guru of the play arranged his harmonium on a small table, exactly in front of the stage, along with a mic and the reading-stand on which he placed his age-old book, containing dialogues and songs for the play. The guru was flanked by other musicians playing instruments like mridangam and bell-plates. The play started with a prayer song offered to Lord Vinayaka. The opening scene was one where *Manthara*, the maid of queen Kaike, enters the queen's bedroom to brainwash the queen against Rama.

Venga sat with Aruna somewhere in the corner of the crowd. This part was always his favourite from *Ramayana*. It was her mother's favourite too. Especially the part where Dasharatha is about to break his own promise made to Kaike, and Rama convinces his father not to do so. He explains how '*the promise he made and the words he uttered, as the king of Ikshvaku dynasty, are sacrosanct. And, in a yuga where the promised word is sacrosanct, breaking it would bring ruins to the king and thenceforth, to the kingdom. If the king falters on his promises, his people would falter on his commands later.*' The part, where Rama's brother Lakshmana joins his brother into exile along with Sita, appeared on the stage. Venga shed a few tears. Even among all the loudspeaker noises, Aruna heard her husband's cry. She asked him if he was fine. He said, "If I had a brother like Lord Rama, I would have accompanied him anywhere like Lakshmana, even in his death." Aruna pleaded with her husband not to speak of the death. She held his head rested it on her lap, and continued watching the drama.

Inside the house, Asobha had woken up to the loudspeakers. Sitting on her bed, she listened to the story. She couldn't prevent herself from relating to the story. "*Was I Kaike or Kousalya to my Rama? Lord Rama succumbed to Kaike's wish. My Rama succumbed to my whims. I wish my Rama also had a Vishwamitra in his life. He could have navigated the hardships of the family as smoothly as Lord Rama did. He would have lived well and died well.*" She pondered all along the play and kept correlating her life with the run of drama. When the moment came for Lord Rama to leave the palace, she fell back into Rama's childhood when he had gone missing for two weeks. The guilt-ridden soul could not avoid but introspect about the moment Rama had returned home after those two weeks. She doubted herself about the worried-face she had that day. She wasn't sure anymore if she had been feeling whatever she emoted, or if she just emoted for the benefit of onlookers. She resented in confusion.

4
The Outcast

Vaisaki was glad that Vanka was not home when Rama was brought back from school after Vaidhe's incident. He had gone to a vegetable mandi in Madras with a load of potatoes which were just harvested. He was to return after two days. Vaisaki thought potatoes had saved her grandson for the time being, and that everyone would forget about that episode by the time Vanka returned. For Rama, waking up the next morning was like any other day. He woke up and went to school. But the school was not the same. He noticed that Vaidhe was absent in the class. He asked one of his classmates why she was not there. The classmate told him that she had taken the transfer certificate from the school and her parents were going to admit her to a town school. The town of Klar was about twenty kilometres from Bani village. But for Rama, Vaidhe had moved further away. He did not even get a chance to ask why her father thought that he was the one who kissed her. However futile it seemed, he wished she was there to tell the world around him he had done no wrong. Most of his classmates, individually and in groups, had kept him at bay. In the eyes of his peers, he had become a constant subject of humiliation and in the eyes of teachers, a continued example of how and what not to be.

A couple of days passed, and Vanka arrived at home. He seemed sad and frustrated. The ladies assumed that the load of potatoes was not sold for a fair price. They kept the school incident from Vanka. They did not want to augment his fury. And Rama too did not have any intention to enrage his uncle. In the evening, Vanka called both Rama and Venga for dinner. Rama stepped out of the room but Venga did not. While Rama sat down on the floor cross-legged with the tumbler in front of him, everyone heard a soft sobbing from the siblings-room. Vanka stood up and went into the room to inquire what was up with Venga. Coming out of the room, he headed straight to the kitchen, grabbed a stick which was supposed to be used to muddle ragi flour, came to the hall where Rama sat expecting food on his plate, twisted Rama's left hand with his left and hit him on the back with no less intent than to break his bones. After taking a few beatings, Rama grabbed the stick which hindered Vanka's incessant blows. Vanka tried to pull the stick out of Rama's grab. But, Rama held the stick tightly with both his hands. That didn't stop Vanka though. He lifted the stick along with the boy, and he started kicking him on the back and the buttocks, into the air. Rama, signalling his failure to stop Vanka, released the stick from his clutch. He kept thrashing the boy, and Asobha remained a mere spectator. Her stomach churned and her eyes cried, but her body made no attempt to move. When she had enough of the sight, she ran and stayed hidden in the kitchen. She had seen it coming and refused to intervene. Vaisaki kept screaming in her feeble voice to let the boy go, to which Vanka paid no heed. The screams of Vaisaki had attracted the people walking close to the house. They clogged near the windows around the house to witness the drama with a peek. They did not venture or feign to interfere, nor did they take leave.

Hearing all the ruckus from the hall, Venga had already come out of his room, and he was witnessing the scene. He seemed to be content with what was happening. For the past two days, he was put through bitter humiliation by his classmates. They tagged him as the 'pervert's brother'. "A pervert's brother can only be a pervert" was the common slogan among his classmates. Unlike Rama, Venga minded words and they were sufficiently irksome. He felt the tinge of each word of humiliation, whether it was truth or trash. He drew rage from every little giggle of his classmates. His narration of the incidents from the school to his uncle and Vanka's compassion for him had taken a toll on Rama that night. Vanka's anger was not just about the school's incident. The frustration he was in, after returning from Madras, was also meted out on Rama. The thrashing was stopped, finally, when Arobha fell and grabbed Rama in her arms. "What devil was stopping you from doing this all the while he was thrashing my boy?" Vaisaki shouted at Arobha. "You never give due consideration for any good deed I do!" Arobha retorted and ordered Rama to run into his room. She calmed her husband. The rage in the house was brought down. Vanka asked Arobha to remove Rama's dinner plate which had remained empty and untouched on the floor.

"Venga, go to your room and get all your belongings for the next two days. Stay in your mother's room," Vanka ordered after the dinner. Venga obeyed. "Aro, bring me a couple of locks from the trunk," Vanka ordered Arobha. She obeyed too. Once Venga shifted his belongings to his mother's room, Vanka went into the room and saw Rama sitting on his bed scribbling something in the notebook. He locked the door, went out of the house and locked the windows of the room from outside. Rama did not understand what was going on until midnight. The head felt slightly dizzy. He woke up to seek some food. He couldn't open the door. He checked the bolt, the door was not locked inside. He knocked on the door calling his mother. Vanka opened the door instead, and asked him, "What do you want?" He replied that he was hungry. Vanka ordered him to stay foodless for two days as a lesson to realise the mistake he had committed. Rama attempted to say that he had made no mistake, but Vanka shut him down before he could reiterate the same thing. "You will be fed when you learn. This is the punishment to put a leash on you. If you try to break the lock and come out anyway, I will up the ante." Vanka warned sternly as he locked the door. Rama called his uncle and asked if he could go to the bathroom. He was let out on watch and brought back in. He was securely locked inside the room again.

With an empty stomach and nothing else to do, Rama sat awake through the night recollecting the evening; his mother's silent hideout, grandmother's futile shoutout, his uncle's fury. But what perplexed him the most was the feeling of content on his brother's face as he was being dragged and thrashed aground. He struggled to come to terms with the crooked look on Venga's face, but in vain. Along with the tendencies of the compelling new-moon night, the mind ran back in time to recollect the memories of his brother. He went back to recalling the play-arena near the Indian Beech tree, where he was struck on the nose by the hit-stone. He remembered his brother crying out loud and whining. He had shown no intent to nurse the wound. He also recalled Kencha, his friend, holding the collar of Varna before others could intervene, and he recalled him offering a hand to stop the bleeding. Venga had stayed away from the blood. The only service he had to offer was tears. He recalled another fight with playmates during a marble game. A fight broke out during the play and Rama was defending himself against the playmate. The playmate's cousin lent a hand to cause a hurdle to Rama's defence. Rama's blood brother, Venga, stood at a distance, screaming, "Leave my brother! Leave him alone!" He recalled many incidents of Venga, pocketing anything that came out of Arobha's special affection, while he shared everything that came out of Vaisaki's special love.

He had no clue what conversation took place between Venga and Vanka earlier that night which prompted his uncle to beat him to a pulp. But the lining-up memories sure gave out a smell of it. The impressions of shared-blood had stopped Rama from seeing the subtleties of emotions vis-a-vis life. More thoughts burnt him up further. The body craved for food, but he had nothing to eat. The pot of water kept in the corner of the room had to quench the hunger of the night. The next day, Vanka stayed at home to make sure the punishment was properly meted out. He did not wish to delegate the job to the empathetic ladies of the house. Rama resisted his hunger. The stomach started to make loud noises. The mouth was drying up after emptying the water in the pot. Giving up his resistance, he sat near the door and called out for food in a feeble voice. When not served, he asked for fruit. When not served, he asked for vegetables. When not served, he asked for a glass of milk. Vanka had foreseen the situation, and he had sent Asobha and Arobha to the farmhouse along with Venga, with the pretext of irrigating the farm lands and clearing out the weeds. Vaisaki was sent off to the mutt. The pleads of the boy went unheeded right into the second night.

Another morning rose, and Vanka woke up. His first thought of the day was of irrigating the paddy in the *kaane*, the hinterland of the village reservoir. The need for assistance made him call out for Arobha. Recalling her absence, he picked the next available option. Anyway, he could not leave Rama behind in the hands of the women who were to return later in the day. Before the ladies came back from their farm lands in the south, Vanka had released Rama from the room and taken him to the *kaane* towards the north of the village. On the way, Rama looked around, swirling his eyes in search of some fruit in the surrounding trees, or some vegetable in the surrounding crop fields. It was the time of the year when the thorny shrubs thrived. The rest of the plants hardly bore any fruit. And it was the time of the season when all the farmers had harvested their crops. As his eyes were about to fatigue into giving up the search, they fell on the flowered Rerani plants among the shrubs bordering the road. He plucked a bunch of flowers and like a hungry bee, sucked the juice out of all of them at once. Walking behind his uncle, the boy continued his parade of surreptitiously plucking a bunch of flowers and sucking the marcels of nectar off of them. The stomach kept his eyes busy. The usual playful rows of tiny ants that were apparent all along the way, evaded his hungry eyes, and so did the people and the cattle, crossing his path. Upon reaching the paddy land, the frightening hefty man ordered Rama to finish irrigating one-third of their fields by the time he irrigated the rest. Luckily, irrigating the paddy fields was much easier than irrigating any other crop. Contemplating his petty luck among all the misery, he thanked his deity and engaged himself in irrigating. Nonetheless, without food for almost two days, the task turned out to be mountainous. He prayed to Hanuman as he shiveringly finished the task.

After finishing the job at hand, he sat down for a respite. Vanka, who had already finished his share of work and was ranting at Rama for his delay, came near to him and offered a pot of water to drink and said, "I have a repair job in the powerhouse. You go home now. Tell your aunt not to bring breakfast for me. I will come home once I am done." Rama took a few steps before he heard his uncle again. "Go straight to the house and stay in your room until I return. Don't kindle with any mischief," he was warned. Rama nodded with a yes and rushed through the fields like a mouse that had escaped from the clutch of a cat. He was finally free and could elevate his attempts to feed the stomach. On his way back, he plucked and sucked the juice out of more and more Rerani flowers. But, the flowers could scent only so much to life. The tiny flowers, all in unison, couldn't satiate him. He sought a fulfilling solution. He ran towards an array of coconut trees. Gazing at the tall trees full of coconuts, he investigated for the smallest among them. He had never climbed a tree before, but he had some experience watching others climb. Though smallest among them, the tree he sought looked sky-high anyway. He grabbed the stem and crawled up slowly. After a few feet, he incessantly gasped for breaths. Whatever strength was left in him was lost, and his arms and legs beckoned to release the grip. As he lost control of the grip, he slid along the length of the stem until the bottom of the tree. The laws of nature wouldn't apply any differently to the innocent. The slide to the bottom had scratched his chest and caused bleeding. In spite of the bleeding, he kept worrying about the torn shirt, in fear of punishment that it could draw from his uncle. In that fear, Rama gave up the idea of trying again for coconuts. As he walked back, he noticed jujube fruits which were yet to ripen, and he decided to give them a shot. He plucked a bunch of them without heeding the pinching of the thorns. After eating a couple of them his throat became sore. He threw away the rest of the bunch in utter despair and walked towards the village. As he approached Madhu Stores, he saw a bunch of bananas hung out for display. He went to the shop and inquired Madhu, "Whose farm did you get the banana fruit from?" He was disappointed to hear that they were bought from far away Klar town, not from any place nearby. "*Anna*, can I take one banana?" he begged. Madhu asked him for fifty paise. Rama said he had no money but promised to pay later.

Madhu was not new to the trickery of kids – putting on innocent faces in order to get the edibles without paying. However, with a torn shirt and feeble voice, Rama didn't look to be tricking. Handing him a banana he said, "Your uncle earns thousands but hesitates to lend even a hundred. Here you are begging for a banana. Play of life! What happened to you?" Swallowing the banana, Rama sighed 'nothing'. Madhu noticed the urge with which Rama engulfed the fruit and he couldn't resist offering one more, and then one more, and more, until he was quenched.

Rama arrived at home, entered his room and closed the door. His mother and aunt were back from the farms and were busy preparing breakfast. Vaisaki was not at home. Venga, who had dressed up for school entered the hall from Asobha's room and shouted, "Amma, breakfast! I am hungry." Asobha served him a hot plate of rice and mixed-vegetable curry. "Your brother is not in his room. Did you see him?" She asked. "How would I know? He might have gone to wander and plunder our honour." Shrugging off his response, she went back to the kitchen. Rama heard his brother from his room. He too shrugged off his brother's response in silence. He tried to sleep on the mat, hoping to catch a respite from everything happening around him. Before he could catch that respite, Vanka arrived. "Where is he?" he asked Arobha, who came running with a towel for his bath. "Who?" she asked. "Son of our clan! The one who is bidding our honour on the street!" he shouted, at which point, Rama woke up and sat down tensed. In a minute, Vanka had intruded into Rama's room and dragged him out by his collar. He repeated his charade of abuse again in the same fashion from the day before. Arobha came running to repeat her charade of offering half-willed resistance to Vanka's action. Meanwhile, Asobha repeated her charade of staying hidden in the kitchen, avoiding the sight of her son getting beaten up – only this time she was eager to know why and hence kept her ears keen. As Arobha continued to offer her resistance, she also kept asking why he was beating the crap out of her nephew. Vanka, who was still busy venting his anger out, did not answer her immediately. Once he was done, he tried to reason with his anger. "That bugger, Madhu! Disgraced me on the road in public." He groaned.

"What came on him?" Arobha asked. "This scoundrel! All because of him! As if he has no one, he has gone begging to that bugger's shop. On my way back, when the entire village was watching, the bastard intentionally called me out, and you know what he said, 'O Vanka, you earn in thousands, but can't even feed a kid at home? What is the use of all the treasure you hold?' Huh! When I held his collar, he revealed the great deed of this scoundrel!" He turned to Rama and continued, "When I was a kid, I have stayed hungry for weeks at times. You can't resist yourself for a couple of days? Dog's life!"

Asobha came rushing out of the kitchen and started slapping Rama continuously. "Why do you do this? Instead, you could as well feed me some poison! I can die peacefully!" She continued slapping. Rama tried to block his face with his hands. At least this time, he knew why he was beaten. But, he had no instinct that feeding himself could be an immoral act and that it could draw such an ire from the family. "He did not bend to my thrashing! There is no use in slap-touching him like that!" Vanka said resentfully and turned to Arobha, "Hey, go inside and bring everything to put chilly-smoke." For a moment, chills ran through Rama's nerves on hearing chilly-smoke. He had only heard it in the stories of his schoolmates. Among all the things that had come up in conversations struck with other kids, he had heard that there was no graver punishment than chilly-smoke. Arobha came carrying a big bowl of aluminium, partially filled with red embers of fine wood. In another hand was a fistful of dried and dreadful red-chillies. Vanka went to Rama's room and brought out a thick woollen rug through which even the air dared not to try escaping. With the rug in one hand, he pulled Rama to the centre of the hall with another hand. Arobha placed the bowl of embers in front of Rama. The rug was unfolded and spread on top of Rama, as well as the bowl, leaving no gap around and along the ground. Vanka held Rama's neck over the rug and pushed his face close to the bowl. The lizard brain in the child resisted the push but could not outdo the strength of a well-built adult. Asobha ran into the kitchen, sobbing. Upon Vanka's signal, Arobha lifted the rug at one end and threw the chillies into the bowl. '*This is it!*' Rama remembered the technique his friends had spoken about, in order to escape the rigour of chilly-smoke. As Arobha's hand lifted the rug, to pour the chillies, Rama took a long breath in, closed his eyes and mouth, blocked his nose with the grip of his fingers, and stayed quiet without breathing. Vanka, who held Rama for a while, was surprised. There was no choking of breath, no cry for respite! He opened the rug to check on him. As soon as the rug was removed, Rama released his nose and breathed out. The uncle, who comprehended the trick, went bizarre. He asked Arobha to bring more chillies. Only this time, he held Rama until he gave up his breath. The raging chilli fumes gushing out of the embers, with nowhere else to go, rushed into the lungs of the child who had just given up holding his breath and had inhaled in search of life. At first, he coughed incessantly. After a few breaths, the chilli fumes choked his throat, rendering him impossible to cough. His body shivered helplessly, like a headless chicken in the hands of a butcher. "Enough! He would die." Arobha sounded worried. Heeding to her, Vanka released the neck of the child and removed the rug. As Rama leaned back, the sweat rolled down through every pore of his skin, and the mucus drooled down from the nose and mouth. The maroon eyes, which had welled up, seemed to be searching for life around. What the eyes failed to find, his breath tried to sense in the air. A sudden gush of air entered his lungs, unchoking his throat. Albeit the burning lungs, he felt a bit of life. Every breath he took kept burning the smoke-filled lungs. But he couldn't stop gasping. Slowly, coming to senses, he looked around for a chance. Mustering all the strength, he fled the house like a gazelle before Vanka could make sense of it. Befooled, Vanka chased him, but in vain. Stopping at the gate, he shouted, "Come back! You will see my wrath. Scoundrel!"

Asobha heard the noise. She came out rubbing the tears, which had done no good for anyone. "Where did he go?" she asked. "Where will he go? He will be back. Don't think too much. Let us go inside." Arobha, who had followed her husband outside the home, calmed down Asobha and took her inside. Rama had escaped from his home. The people on the street had the spectacle of a show. Some people on the street felt pity for Rama, after all, he was just about eight years old, and he was a kid who was adored until recently.

For the boy who had to escape from the dire clutches of his own family, the milieu around him was as meaningless as his own home. He ran away from the sight of everyone. He ran a furlong, amid the burning lungs. Noticing that no one was following him, he gave up running and walked. An involuntary mind often chooses a familiar path. He walked a mile in the direction of the family farm fields. And, he walked, in utter confusion, on the same roads which were once walked by his father, with utter clarity and joy. He crossed the farm fields, crossed Bani and reached the neighbouring village, Koti. As soon as he sat down under a tree, he dozed off. And, later in the evening, he was woken up by the mist. He moved under the arch of the nearby Hanuman temple. He was too young to ponder over the next course of his life, nor did he have enough strength to ponder over. Sleep caught hold of him again as he laid down on the floor, in the lap of Hanuman.

In the morning, he opened his eyes to the wall of the temple. Reminiscence of sleeping in his room was lingering in his drowsy head. He tried to cover up his legs with the blanket, but he could not reach it. As he wondered why his mattress felt harder than usual, he came to his senses. Waking up from the floor, he prostrated to Hanuman, praying for the courage to be alone. The sun was on the horizon. He felt no burning in the lungs. The dullness had evaded his mind. He went to the nearby well and cleaned himself up. He drank a bounty of water, plucked a neem stalk, crushed one end of it and brushing his teeth with it, walked towards the pond of Koti.

At home, on the previous night, Vaisaki had a meaningless fight with Vanka. She urged him to bring back her grandson. Vanka did not budge. He was motivated to defend his action citing the silence of Rama's mother. "His mother sees no wrong in my action! What is your problem? Where can he go? He has to come back home, tonight or later. If you can stay patient and keep your mouth shut for some time, everything will be alright!" he shouted at Vaisaki. She started blaming Asobha's heart for its rigidity and silence, while she repeated her blame on Vanka for outcasting a progeny of the family. Asobha muttered, "It's for his own good. If he stays out for a couple of days, he will learn the value of family and how to honour it. Anyway, he is just eight. He is bound to come back." Vaisaki retorted, "If you treat him this way at this age, he will learn to live without you, without a family. Have you thought of that? The way Vanka has treated him after his father's death and the way the entire family has turned against him today, why would he come back? A kid is bound to run back to his family only when he is bound by emotions and love. If you deprive him of them, he will obviously pursue them elsewhere." Asobha's heart started to pound in fear. She wondered if she had played the game of teaching the kid a lesson – on honour and family values, through abandonment – for too far and too long. When Rama did not return home for dinner, she asked Vanka to go – along with neighbours, Kedara and Jagga – in search of her kid. The three of them took three different directions in search of Rama. By the time they covered every nook and corner of the village, it was pitch-dark and exhausting. To the dismay of Asobha, they returned home empty-handed. Vanka attempted to assure Asobha that they would look for him the next day. Asobha was reluctant. But, she couldn't do anything by herself either. Waiting for the next morning, she went to sleep, pondering the whereabouts of her boy. The poultry shed at their farm fields; a few temples in and around the village; relatives' and acquaintances' houses in the village; and several other places popped into her mind as the probable places where Rama could be found. When she was about to sleep, she heard the rooster-call. Waking up early in the morning with no sleep, she went and knocked on Vanka's door and called him out. It was still dark outside. As he came out, still sleepy, she asked him to resume the search for Rama immediately. Vanka wore his sweater, took a torch light, gathered Kedara and Jagga and went out of the village looking for Rama.

Vanka took the road to the south, Kedara to the east and Jagga to the north. Most of the search was done on a bicycle and to a certain extent, on foot. Nonetheless, by noon, all the three returned exhausted. Vaisaki was fed up with the namesake of a search party. She asked Vanka to report to the police. He looked hesitant. He was a little afraid that, if questioned and found, police may bash him for pushing the kid to run away. Vaisaki grasped his concern. She turned to Kedara and asked him to take Asobha to the police station. Blaming Asobha for failing to stop Vanka's brutality as a mother, she asked her to go to the police as redemption and tell whatever story she had to say, but lodge a missing complaint. She just wanted her grandson to return home.

The registered complaint stated that the 'kid was begging for food in a shop on the village street; as a punishment, the mother and the uncle asked the boy to seek forgiveness from the shop vendor; the boy who went to ask forgiveness did not return home; the family which waited until dinner, searched for him in the entire village all through the night; after continuing the search on the next day, until noon and upon failing to find him, lodged a complaint in the police station.' When Asobha returned home, Vanka read the copy of the complaint and took a respite. The police started their search with a preliminary inquiry in the neighbourhood. Ruling out the village, they started to look out.

Thirteen days later, he was reported as a missing kid by a temple sevak to the temple administration during a grand procession at *Avaleshwara* temple, Avali. When the temple administration announced his name along with the village details on the loudspeakers, a couple from Bani took note of it and approached the temple administration. However, the boy failed to recognise them. Incidentally, the police sub-inspector, who had registered the missing complaint and who was at the temple for the procession, took note of the announcement too, and he approached the temple office room. The police, after informing the couple from Bani that he couldn't send the kid with them, assured the temple administration that he would deliver the boy to his family by himself. By that evening, Rama was back at home, but as a different person altogether.

5
Two Widows

It had been almost six months since Raju's demise. Rama had started to toddle. And, Venga was in his mother's womb, about to be thrown open into the wilderness. Asobha had been to her parents' home in Katilu, where she was offered special care – tailored for pregnancy. Her mother, Lacchu, had taken her home as soon as she had come to know of the conception. It had been public news from day one. Asobha had thrown up in front of all the women who had gathered in the hall on the Eleventh-Day ritual of her husband. Upon holding her pulse, the doctor confirmed the pregnancy, and upon completion of the ritual, Lacchu and Vengappa convinced Vaisaki to take her home with them. Asobha's parents had just started to look out for a suitable match for their son, Atura. But, they postponed the matchmaking to accommodate their grieving daughter, and most importantly, to offer their full attention to care for the pregnant lady. She got the best treatment at home during this pregnancy, better than during the birth of Rama. If Raju was looking over, he would have envied his in-laws.

Vengappa ordered Atura to decorate the house with bunches of tulsi and Chrysanthemum every day. Lacchu helped her daughter in taking the daily baths, and later, she dried the hair with *samrani* smoke. She took care of washing Asobha's clothes and keeping her room tidy. With time, she became part and parcel of Asobha's life, until the pregnancy. She also performed *vrathas* and offered *poojas* every day, keeping her daughter and the baby in prayers. Asobha too prayed to God, as was the custom, to bring a healthy life into her womb, which would bring honour unto her family. She was always served the desired food in its best form. She was not coerced into eating, and at the same time, she was not let to stay hungry too. Lacchu made sure that Asobha was fed, even if it meant cooking a couple more times to satisfy her taste. "Vengadi family has no dearth of caring. Treat my daughter so well that she would forget the pampering received by her spouse's house during the first pregnancy." Vengappa had ordered the family on the first day she arrived. "Should you tell a mother how to take care of her daughter?" Lacchu's teasing rhetoric had brought out a new vigour in the pregnant lady who had just lost her husband. Asobha was overwhelmed by everything that was offered on her behalf. But she could not resist missing the overwhelming tolerance and patience of Vaisaki. Pregnancy is the ultimate test of a family's patience. And Lachhu was patient, no doubt. But at times, when calm and pondering, Asobha could feel the uneasiness of her mother in dealing with her. She would often recall Vaisaki. She had served her with the same devotion with which she had been serving her deity. Perhaps, that is why, when the boy was born, she had not even flinched a bit in choosing to name him 'Rama'.

Vashike, the ceremony for the pregnant woman intended to receive blessings from mothers of the village, was arranged in grandeur as she neared the delivery date. Vaisaki, who had attended the ceremony, remembered how grand that function was when Asobha had carried Rama over a year back. She exchanged a look and a smile with Asobha, who was sitting quietly, recollecting the same past. This time, it was the turn of the mothers from Katilu, to take charge of the event. They filled the place with their plates full of edibles, sarees, flowers, betel leaves and nuts, vermillion and turmeric powders. They sang songs – some welcoming life into their world, some praising God for the gift of the womb bestowed upon women, some seeking the blessings to face the time of birth and the time thereon, and some more in praise of women who bear the brunt of God in the process of offering a new life. The folk songs went on rendering both the tales of child-bearing and teachings of child-rearing. The old women sang with fervour while the young attempted to stay in sync, trying to mouth the words from the old. Despite all the customs being met, the energy among the crowd lacked lustre. Everyone was dressed well, but the place had a dearth of chitter-chatter. Everyone brought all the customary offerings, but the faces had a dearth of laughs and teasing. Everyone sang songs, but the pitch had a dearth of jubilance. The gathered folk weren't sure how to behave with Asobha, given her husband had just died. They had to be mindful, even while blessing her and her baby with a prosperous life. Whomsoever sprinkled blessing-grains on her head uttered their blessing, carefully choosing the words. They blessed her to have a prosperous life with family, but not without wondering how she would achieve it with no spouse. Sitting among the audience, Vaisaki could feel everything which was missing in the aura. She had experienced the same when she was pregnant with Rupini.

When the moment came, the baby had to be delivered at home itself. The village doctor who visited home that night called out instinctively and the baby was delivered within the confines of the Vengadi home. The grandfather, Vengappa, was standing outside the house whispering two names on his lips, one for each gender. When the doctor confirmed it was a boy, he screamed in happiness, "Venga is born!" He named his grandson after himself and after the great 'Kubja Vengadi'. Asobha was not very fond of the archaic name, but she did not want to break her father's excitement. Especially, after letting her firstborn be named by her in-law. Vengappa was waiting to name Arobha's child. But before Arobha could conceive, Asobha did it again and Venga was born. Vengappa had relinquished his wait and quenched his desire to name a grandchild after him with a grand shrill.

Upon hearing the news, Vaisaki visited Katilu's home the next day. Seeing Asobha with a baby in her lap and another one crawling everywhere, she could not resist bringing out the memories of her early motherhood days, when she had to bring up three kids alone. Without the father, the kids always looked scattered and lost. And, the challenges varied between the upbringing of her boys and the girl, Rupini. The boys perhaps had missed their father during their first walk, or first talk, or first day at school, or first time on a bike, etc. But, Rupini had missed her father much more, much earlier, and rather, in a nuanced way, than her brothers. Also, from day one, looking up to her brothers instead of her father had been a difficult task for Rupini, given their mischief and aloofness. Vaisaki had to strike a balance between a mother and a father. She also had to strike a balance between the caretaker and the bread-earner. With very little help here and there, from the neighbours in the village, the struggle had become the reality of her life. The breather was that Shunka had left behind enough land for her to get into farming and a few allied activities. The reminiscence of all the money, owed to her husband by the villagers was erased with his demise, as Shunka had kept his lending privy to himself. However, she had carefully kept each and every paper she found in her husband's vault for any purpose that would befall in the later time; fortunately, the collection included the papers belonging to the farm land. It was sufficiently reliable for her to stand on her own, and keep the encroachers at bay. She had to learn farming, and she farmed whatever tiny piece of her land that she could with her muscles. With the money from the vault, she bought a small pack of poultry and sheep. She also had several saplings of teak, silver oak and sandalwood, planted for the benefit of the far future. She also had bought two cows which provided milk for the family. The excess was sold to the dairy co-operative, earning her a few extra bucks. Only a meagre amount of money flowed in from all the avenues she had, but it was enough to finance the needs of her family.

After almost thirty years, she saw herself in Asobha. With Rama on one side taking slippery steps and Venga on the other, barely opening his eyes in her lap, Asobha drew all the compassion from her mother-in-law. Vaisaki took a respite in the fact that Asobha had people around her to cater to her, and her children's needs. Most importantly, folks from her birth-home. Unlike Asobha, Vaisaki's birth-home had relinquished their bond with her a few days after her marriage, owing to a fight that broke out between her father and her husband over a trivial matter. "*It isn't the same with Asobha. Especially after Raju's demise, the Vengadi family had grown closer to their daughter. Also, her blood sister is her co-sister. Vanka too is potential support for the children, if need be, even if he is to have his own children in the later part of his life,"* Vaisaki thought. And herself, she made up a solemn mind to contribute as much as she could, to her grandchildren, until her last breath.

She had come with Arobha and Vanka to visit her new grandson. She suppressed the display of too much love on the eve of having a second grandchild, as she recalled the whisperings of the disgruntled younger daughter-in-law when the first one was born. Though her happiness was overwhelming, she wore a facade of calmness to avoid envying Arobha any further. But every action has unintended repercussions. Asobha, who noticed that Vaisaki was not as thrilled with her second child, made space for whispers in her mind. *'Why is she not thrilled? Is it because my parents named him with my family name? Or does this boy remind her of her son's death?'* In her shackles of thoughts, she blamed destiny for putting her through such a fate and for ruining one of the best days of her life. From her deep shackles, Asobha was woken up by Vaisaki, asking for Rama. Asobha told her that he might be playing with his grandparents. Vaisaki went out of the room looking for Rama. She heard his voice from the kitchen and called him dearly. Lacchu, who was busy preparing coffee for the guests, lifted and dropped him off at the kitchen door, pointing at Vaisaki, "Look, look... Vaiamma has come! Go and hug her!" As she released him, he ran a weird stride with his tiny feet while smiling at Vaisaki. Halfway, he stumbled upon his toe and fell down. He hit his head on the leg of the wooden table. He did not cry but started rubbing a spot on his head. Vaisaki hurried to him, took him into her lap and rubbed his head where he had placed his fingers. Not sure if it was for recalling her son so much on that day, or for the way her son had died, or for the way Rama injured himself, or due to all those reasons, the events from the day of her son's death flashed in her mind.

6
Slip of a Moment

Raju woke up at his usual time in the early morning, unleashed the cattle and followed them on their walk to the farm field. At the field, he tied them to a tree with a long rope in an open meadow where they mulched on the fresh green grass. He filled buckets with water from the farm tank, mixed *indi* and *busa* into it, and placed one bucket each for each cow and buffalo. He went around inspecting the state of the crops. While returning after the inspection, he noticed the tamarind trees full of ripened fruit. He had been waiting for a couple of weeks, without knowing what to do with that yield. If he had to sell the crop to a contractor, he would only get seven-hundred rupees per tree. However, if he could pluck the tamarinds himself and sell them in the market, he would make close to a thousand rupees per tree. In that case, he would have to spend around three-hundred rupees per tree, for the labour. He was trying to find cheap labour to finish the job at a much lower price. His attempts had gone in vain. It was very tough to find cheap labour during a fine season of tamarinds, and that too with high prices in the market.

Looking at the trees, Raju concluded that it was better if he himself did the job. Anyway, there were only three trees. He gave a moment of thought. If he started thrashing tamarinds that day, he could be done with all three trees within a week, even while attending to other work. He went into the farm-shed and brought out the ready-made stick to thrash the tamarinds. He also carried a sickle with him. It had been a few years since he last did such work. Sticking the stick on his back into the shirt, and holding the sickle by his mouth, he climbed the tree via a low-hanging branch. Slowly, he walked along the branch and reached the central trunk of the tree from where it had spread all around. He inspected the branches for a while, and then chose the high-hanging branch at the centre to start with, and from there, decided to go to his right, in rounds and later downwards, covering the entire tree. He finished the top branch in a few minutes. Moving to his right, he kept thrashing the tamarinds off the branches. "What brother? You have climbed yourself? Didn't find any labour?" Vanka, who was passing the tree on his way to the powerhouse, shouted. Raju asked him to take a stick and sickle and climb onto another tree. Vanka responded that he had to pump the water to the tomato crop before they lost electricity. He assured that he would join once he finished irrigating, and rushed to the powerhouse, a few furlongs away.

Raju continued to clear tamarinds off their branches. At places, he stuck the sickle to the stick and scraped off the fruits which otherwise could not be thrashed. Right from his teenage years, he had a habit of making sure that every single tamarind had fallen to the ground from the branches that he touched. By sunrise, he had cleared most of the top region and was exhausted. In his teen days, he used to climb down only when he was done with half the tree, by which time his mother would usually arrive with the breakfast basin. As he had been out of touch from the hard labour for quite some time, he tired early and there was no breakfast either. He thought of finishing his current branch and then getting down to quench his thirst. As he walked to the edge, he held the branch above with his left hand. Carefully sliding his feet along the branch he stood on, he reached to the bunch of tamarinds situated at the tip of the branch using the sickle stuck to the stick, firmly held in his right hand. He pulled the stick in an attempt to cut the tamarind bunch. The hard stalk of the branch held the sickle, and the sickle slipped from the grip of the stick sliding to the edge of it. Raju jerked instantly in an attempt to stop the sickle from falling out of the stick and lost his balance. The legs slipped from the branch he stood on. Letting the stick off his right hand, he used the other hand too to get a quick grip on the holding branch. But, it was a quick slip of a moment, and his falling weight broke the tiny branch that supported him. Raju fell down, holding the broken branch in his hands, from about twenty feet high. As he was at the top, close to the centre of the tree, he was just above the thicker branches spreading out from the trunk. He fell, scratching and hitting all the branches along his downfall, and he finally hit a thick branch with the back of his head, breaking his skull open. The last hit to his head provided a sudden torque to his falling body, and it spun him a round or two before he fell to the ground, head first, breaking his neck, skull and a few bones.

A squeaky noise started emanating from under the tree and spread across the area. The noise sounded like a peacock's cry. And, the area was full of peacocks and peahens. The very few people, who were at work in their respective fields on that early morning – including Vanka, who heeded the voice, did not attribute it to that of a dying man. As the voice went undying for several minutes, Jagga, who was ploughing his land nearby, paid attention. The voice, which started to die down, sounded more like a human cry. As Jagga approached the tamarind tree, he was jolted by the sight of a human bleeding into the earth in the merciless shadow. Waking up from disbelief, he started crying out for help. Hearing his hue and cry which did sound like a human voice, Vanka, Sheshu and Bala, ran to the tree. By that time, Jagga had already inspected the injury. He had seen the open skull at the back of the head. As he lifted the head, the blood dripped like tap water. Worst of all, Raju was still conscious. Raju could feel the blood gushing out of the rest of his body except for the head. The back of the head had gone numb for him. And he was utterly paralysed. "Jagga, do something! Please do something, brother!" Raju begged and cried. Jagga used his towel to press the wound, but it was not helpful. He placed Raju's head back on the ground with his towel as a cushion. "Help me, Vanka. I can't move my limbs. I can't turn my neck. I can't even feel my head!" Raju cried upon seeing his brother. Vanka stood still in disbelief. Jagga, taking notice of the dumbstruck brother, shouted and asked him to go and fetch a vehicle. Sheshu pitched in. He rushed to the shed at his farm to bring his truck. Vanka slowly moved towards his brother. As he came close, Raju felt the severity of his fall in the eyes of Vanka rather than through his own pain. Vanka held his brother's hand and sat beside him. Looking at the mutilation of the body, he blabbered in search of a word, to console his brother. He kept rubbing the hand and the forehead every now and then. "Water, water! Somebody throw me a sip of water!" Raju begged. Jagga kept feeding him a sip of water whenever he asked for it.

In a minute, Sheshu came back driving his truck. In it was a tarpal sheet. Sheshu spread the sheet on the ground. Vanka and Jagga lifted and slowly placed Raju onto the tarpal and shifted him into the truck. Jagga sat beside Raju, cushioning the broken head with his thigh and pressing the cracked skull with the towel, still attempting to stop the bleeding. Vanka sat on the other side, placing Raju's legs on his thighs, and rubbing his feet all along the way. Bala was sent to Raju's home in order to inform the family of the incident and to bring them near the town hospital. Sheshu drove the truck straight to the hospital. Upon reaching the hospital, the duty doctor performed first aid and initial assessment and informed that such critical patients could not be treated at that hospital. "We are not equipped to treat such grave cases," he said. He advised them to immediately shift the patient to the neighbouring city hospital. They provided the hospital ambulance with a ventilator. A doctor and a nurse accompanied them. On the way, the doctor tried to ventilate and resuscitate the patient. However hard he tried, they could only make it halfway to the city before Raju succumbed to his injuries.

Meanwhile, Bala had brought Asobha, Arobha and a couple of their neighbours to the town hospital in his tractor. Asobha got down from the tractor trolley and ran to the hospital with a huge cry. Upon inquiring, the dilapidated woman was told that the patient was sent to the city hospital in an ambulance. The duty doctor asked them to wait close by, and that he would inform them of the patient's status as soon as they heard from the city hospital. The doctor was expecting a call from his staff, soon after reaching the destination.

Bala saw Sheshu's truck parked out at the emergency ward. As Asobha and Arobha waited inside, Bala took the others to inspect the vehicle for blood residue. The floor of the truck was marooned. They discussed the chance of his survival based on the residual blood left in the truck. After speculating it as a one-in-a-million chance, they returned to Asobha and Arobha. Bala offered to bring coffee for Asobha, but she refused. After a few minutes, an ambulance entered the hospital gate and moved towards the mortuary. The staff, who took note of the ambulance, called Asobha and her group. Pointing to the ambulance, the staff informed them that it was the same ambulance which had taken the patient to the city hospital.

While Asobha and Arobha pondered on the implication of such an early return, Bala and the neighbours who had inspected the blood residue had already come to a conclusion. The ladies, who were not aware of the meaning of 'mortuary' on the display board, moved towards it in silence. Bala, who already concluded that Raju was dead, whispered to another lady that that was the place where dead bodies were taken. Overhearing the whisper, Asobha's heart jumped for a second. She ran towards the ambulance. As she got closer to it, the door opened and Vanka got down along with the rest of the people inside. They pulled the body out. Asobha stood in dread, witnessing her husband's blue face. There were no tears, there was no cry. Only stillness.

Raju was cremated, and all the post-cremation rituals were carried out by his year-old son Rama, with the aid of Vanka. The mind which grasped no word or custom in the rituals, followed his mother and uncle's instructions obediently till the end of the Eleventh-Day ceremony. Vanka seated the child on his lap and holding his hand, he helped him carry out every ritual. The mantras were uttered by him on behalf of Rama. After the Eleventh-Day rituals, just after everyone had had lunch, Asobha was found to be pregnant with her second child. As Asobha touched her belly and tried to smile, recovering from her loss, Arobha was disgruntled by the envy in her belly. Vanka was in his own world. After witnessing his brother's gruesome death first hand and having foreseen his responsibilities going forward, he had no time for envy in his mind. All he could think was that there would be another child for him to toil for. He contemplated the avenues to save his face at the duty of bringing up two boys, both of whom were not his, in spite of his own barren marriage.

7
The Last Piece

The police dropped Rama at the door steps. His mother received him. The woman, who had always displayed her love for that kid through anger, instead, in the presence of policemen and onlookers, chose to display it differently. The emotions came out gushing through her eyes as soon as she saw him with the police at the door. The hugging, kissing, crying and swearing to not lose him again. Rama stayed calm and remained utterly silent. After the formalities of the reunion, police left the place. Asobha tried to feed him a plate full of food. He did not touch a grain. He said he was not hungry. She tried to solace him and feed him again. He refused. Vaisaki entered the house from the temple. As soon as he saw his grandmother, he ran to her and hugged her. Asobha was a little disappointed at his dispassion towards her. She brushed away her disappointment with the reasoning that he was still in a state of shock from going missing for two weeks. He finished his third and fourth grades at the school with no hindrance from the family. But his teachers at school were not so kind. In their eyes, he still carried the sin of discontinuing a girl from her education and ruining her life. Vaidhe's father, Jana, after sending her to a different school for some time, had stopped her schooling out of his doubt. He was doubtful of such an incident occurring again and he wanted his daughter to maintain respect in the society rather than attaining education. When Suneena tried to persuade him to send her daughter to school, he said, "If she retains honour and respect until marriage-age, someone will come and marry her. If she loses them, no one will even sniff her, even with any number of degrees." Vaidhe was paying her due with her life.

The wounds left by Vaidhe were still daunting in school. From that day, teachers had started evaluating his answers and assignments thoroughly and prejudicially. He failed to score well without being explained why. He was pushed back to the corner in every grade seating. Some teachers even went to the extent of giving him extra work, physical or academic. The science teacher took things a few steps further. Being his class teacher, she wanted to make an example out of him. From the day of Vaidhe's incident, she made him stand outside the class in a chicken-shape – with head bent to the knee and hands holding the ears, being wrapped from around and under the thighs. She dragged this daily ordeal for a couple of months. Her desire to see a tear in his ears was never fulfilled. The unfulfilled desire to see his tears only made him a worse culprit in her eyes.

Day by day, Rama could feel the futility of his presence in the class, better and better. He started bunking classes of his inconvenience or the classes to which he thought he might be an inconvenience. Whenever he skipped classes, he tried to fill the time-gap by visiting the open tent to watch a movie or a drama. By the end of fourth grade, he had failed in three subjects. But by then, he had watched seven movies and ten stage dramas. By the end of fifth grade, he had failed in four subjects and came close in the rest, and had watched fifty-two movies and around twenty-five stage dramas. In addition to that, his grandmother's stories and epics were a daily affair. Every night after dinner, his grandmother would narrate parts of puranas, Ramayana and Mahabharata. After listening to a significant part of them, he would ask her to tell about a person in detail, from the epics. Every night a different persona. He would ask questions in between – moral, emotional and sometimes just for fun. Like a mirror, she would answer all his questions with the same fervour.

By the time he was eleven, his only friend, both from the school and the village, left him. Sixth grade had barely started. A teacher in his class announced that Kencha had cleared an exam he had written half a year back. It was an entrance test to some famous school called Navodaya. The teacher looked to be proud of him, just like Drona was proud of Arjuna when the latter spotted and took down the bird's eye from the tree while he was a kid. Rama was nothing but happy to hear his friend being praised. But, within a week, the void that Kencha had left became apparent in his life. In the first year of his stay in Navodaya, Kencha met him during Dussehra and summer holidays and shared a lot of tales from his new-land, where he met a variety of students all over from different places. From the next year onwards, when Kencha's family shifted to a faraway town, Malur, the meetings stopped. However, the letters kept arriving through post. Month by month, and year by year, the count of letters surged down, and later the count of words. Rama learnt to grow more and more alone. He stopped going home during the lunch break. Instead, everyday afternoon, he walked to the Hanuman temple of Koti; sat there in silence for a while or climbed the Flamboyant tree beside the temple; plucked a green pod and a couple of ripened flower-buds; got down and sat on the granite bench; ripped open the pod at the sutures using a stone; peeled the seed one by one, slowly removed the rubber; ate the rubber; and after finishing the seeds, peeled off the ripened bud; plucked a couple of filaments, cut at their base; held a filament in each hand; fought the filaments, head to head, until one chopped of the anther from another; played until all but one filament was left at the end; declared it the winner and placed it inside the pocket; took a nap when done playing; woke up and returned to school upon hearing the loud bell from the school. This was his daily lunch break. His mother and aunt tried to make him come home for lunch regularly, by scolding and by force but got tired of his ignorance and gave up trying after a while. For a boy who had just lost the only friend to speak to, the freedom to be himself, for a brief time of the day, had come as a gift. When Flamboyant had no flowers or seeds, he visited nearby trees and farm fields, wherever the flowers and fruits were borne. Fresh fruits and vegetables were his new lunch, and the time away from the confines of the classroom was his play time.

One afternoon, as he lay on a branch of a jamun tree eating the fresh fruit at the arm's reach, one of his classmates came looking for him. He called Rama from under the tree to inform him that the principal was looking for him. As he reached the principal's chamber, just after his classmate, he heard the classmate reporting his whereabouts to the principal. The principal started bashing Rama for going out of campus during lunch hours. He questioned him about his persistent absence at home during lunch hour, and also about not bringing a box to school and having lunch with his peers. Rama stayed still, just wondering when the principal started to worry about his whatabouts and whereabouts. The principal later informed that Rama's uncle had come to school, and he was looking for the brothers. He also told him why. Rama immediately started running towards his home. His uncle and brother were not found. Hearing a sound from the kitchen, he hurried there. His mother was cleaning utensils, looking dull. As soon as she saw him, she shouted in her usual angry voice, asking him why he did not go to the hospital with his uncle. He questioned what happened to his grandmother. "Grandma fainted at the door all of a sudden, and however we tried, she did not get up. So, your uncle and aunt took her to the town hospital. She was murmuring your name continuously. On the way, when they were near your school, they wanted to pick up both of you," she said. On hearing that, Rama became cold, stood like ice and was deaf to her further words. He slowly walked into grandma's room and sat down in a corner. The room was dark without the lamp. Holding the crossed knees by his arms, he rested his head on the knees in silence.

In the evening, his uncle came home for dinner, and to carry some in the container for Arobha, who stayed back with the old lady at the hospital. Venga had returned home with his uncle. After the dinner, Rama asked his mother if his uncle could take him to the hospital. He stood near the main door as Asobha went to hand out the carrier to Vanka. He could barely hear what Asobha was saying. After Asobha said her words, Vanka shouted. "Why? When I wanted to take him, he was roaming around. Now he wants to come? Let him come in the morning. Anyway, if I take him now, I have to come back to drop him, and again return to the hospital." Rama heard his uncle's voice loud and clear. Though he was sure that his uncle would say something sore, he had hoped that he would take him. The hope was struck down. The disappointed boy went back to his grandma's room and slept quietly.

He was woken up in the morning by the rumbling voices in the house. Vanka sounded hasty, and he was asking Asobha to prepare the breakfast fast. Rama woke up, ran to the bathroom, finished his morning ablutions, came back, dressed up quickly, went to the hall and whispered to his mother for breakfast. After the carrier was packed for the hospital, Vanka took it and rushed out without minding his nephew. Rama called his mother out and asked her to recommend again to his uncle to take him along. After Asobha's persuasion, Vanka gave a place to Rama on his Luna. It was the first time he ever rode with his uncle on the bike, and it was also the first time ever he visited the Klar town, or any town, except when he was born in that same town, in the hospital. He had seen it though in the stories of some of his friends, especially Kencha.

As the Luna entered the town, the cacophony disturbed Rama's mind. And the sight of the town filled awe on his face. He had seen so many people only in temple fairs and processions before. And, he was witnessing such a long array of houses and buildings. The road went on forever, zig-zagging and criss-crossing. In his village, one had to take a maximum of three turns to reach from one corner to any other. Here, he wasn't sure if the hospital was ever going to arrive. He covered his mouth and nose with his palm to avoid the dust. When they entered the hospital, the smell of ethanol from the floor pinched and signatured in his nose.

The grandmother lay asleep on a cot with white sheets, and one covering her body above up unto the neck. There was some pipe which seemed to bifurcate at the nose and made its way into her nostrils. There was another pipe patched with a tape on her forearm. Arobha received him in her arms and then arranged a chair for him to sit near his grandma's head. She tried to wake her up in the name of his arrival. "*Athhe*, Rama is here." Vaisaki's eyelids opened slowly and the eyeballs moved around in the welled-up water. She slowly turned towards her right, heeding to the hand gesture Arobha was making. She barely heard what Arobha was saying. As she turned to Rama's face, she smiled and said in a feeble voice, "Rama!!" The lady, who on the day before, had been narrating a fable from Mahabharata in varying pitches and voices, was struggling to call his name. He did not expect to see his grandmother in that state. He was a little confused and uncomfortable too. Arobha noticed his silence and urged him to speak something to the old lady. "What are these pipes for, grandma?" he asked. "They are to keep me smiling," she replied. He looked more confused. Before he could ask more weird questions, Arobha intervened and told her how Asobha also wanted to visit but she could not as they needed someone to take care of house chores, and also Venga. As she kept her blabber going on, Vaisaki got bored and turned to Rama again. She remembered something. She crawled her hands into the sheet and searched for something at her waist. The cotton bag and the key, which she always kept stuck into the saree at her waist, were missing. She turned back to Arobha. Arobha got the gist of her look and handed over the cotton bag and the key.

"I have kept some edibles and a box of coins in the almirah. You take them. After that, you hand over the key to your mother," she said and handed over the key to him. She placed her palm into one of the pouches in the bag, searched the pouch with her fingers and then pulled something out. A couple of dried betel leaves and a one-rupee currency note came out. She gave the rupee note to him and placed the leaves back into the pouch. He smiled at the one-rupee note.

He had seen a one-rupee note several years back. When the rupee coins came into his life, the notes went disappearing. A few weeks back, when she was narrating a story from her childhood, she had informed him how his father Raju used to buy one sheep for sixteen annas which was equivalent to one rupee in the later time currency; and she showed four-anna coins which opened his eyes in awe. Such annas were never seen to be used by anyone in his time. He was puzzled at how something that was of value a while ago was lying worthless now. After grandmother's story, he felt the urge to collect anything akin to a four-anna coin, and he recalled the one-rupee note, which he used to often see a few years back, and for some reason, was not to be seen anywhere later. He inquired in shops and asked any person he knew who could hold more than one rupee in the pocket or the saree knot. He had failed to find one. His grandma was one of the first he inquired with. She did not possess it at that point. But later, she had found one and had saved it in her bag to hand it over to Rama. His joy of having one rupee was priceless to that old lady; just what she expected. They talked for a little while. The attendant came in and asked the visitors to leave. "Don't forget to open the red-flowered box from the almirah," she said to him as he started walking away from her.

On one side, the joy of the rupee note, and on the other side, the excitement to see what was in the red-flowered box. The grandmother seemed more exciting and intriguing when in the hospital. '*Maybe, because of the pipes,*' he thought, and slid the note and key into his pocket, and walked out of the hospital. As soon as they stepped out of the hospital, Vanka grabbed the almirah key from him, sternly warned him not to tell his mother anything about the key, and asked him to climb the back of Luna. He obeyed with little contention that at least the rupee note was spared.

As soon as he reached home, he took his book and pencil and started sketching the rupee note. Meanwhile, Vanka looked out for Asobha. When he noticed that she was cleaning the backyard, he entered Vaisaki's room, opened the almirah, inspected it, took out all the jewels and valuables, locked the almirah back and shifted the jewels into the bureau in his room. He also had the internals of the coin box and the red-flowered box checked. He did not find anything of value to him. He left them both inside and intact. He returned to the hospital, and later in the night, he came back home in a black van. Arobha was back with him. Rama and Venga heard the cracking diesel-engine noise and went outside to peek a look. Vanka got down from the van. Arobha followed him out, but she was looking sad, with her eyes welled up. She was covering her mouth with the saree-edge to hide the mewling. The driver came around the van, opened the back door and pulled something out. It seemed like a person sleeping. Vanka helped the driver by lifting it on the other side. They shifted the body onto a wooden cot inside the compound of the house. After seeing the face of the person from close enough, Rama called out loudly for his mom. Asobha hurried out of the house. Everyone from the family had their moment of sorrow and grief. Vanka went into the village to make arrangements for the funeral while others continued their saga of bereaving. After a while, Vanka called Asobha inside and asked her if she possessed the key to Vaisaki's almirah as he wanted to see if the old lady had kept any cash inside, and that he could use it for the funeral arrangements. She said no. He took her inside and broke open the lock in front of her. Both were searching the almirah and inspecting each of the boxes from inside when Rama walked in on them. Vanka was worried for a moment. Rama asked for a red-flowered box and the coin box which his grandma had informed him about. Vanka handed both of them to him without hesitation. Asobha protested a little not to hand over the coin box. He calmed her by informing her that he had peeked into the box, and the coins inside were annas from the old days and held no value.

Rama carried both the boxes to his room and opened the coin box first. He spread out a loin cloth on the floor and poured all the coins from the box onto the cloth. He started picking one by one. There were many denominations of old coins. One-anna, two-anna, four-anna, eight-anna, five-paisa, ten-paisa, twenty-paisa, twenty-five-paisa, fifty-paisa, etc. Also, some of the denominations were present in different shapes and metals. Even in the midst of bereavement, he was left with something to rejoice. He filled the coins back into the box. Now, the turn for the red-flowered box whose contents he was not aware of. It felt light as expected, as it was a very small box. He tried to guess what was inside by moving the box around in his hands, weighing and shaking to hear the sound of the contents inside. Finally, he opened the box. A small stick was stuck to a big *tamarind-candy*. It was at least five times the size of the usual balls of candy she always gave him. He took the candy by the stick, opened his mouth wide open, and swallowed the candy. With eyes shut, he savoured the blast of taste inside his mouth and pulled it out. He recalled discussing his confusion in naming it tamarind-candy with his grandma. He was not very happy about it being named just after tamarind which was the main item used.

He felt the naming was unfair because, just the lump of tamarind, from whichever tree he collected it, did not taste anything close to the candy from his grandmother. "*Even without tamarind also, you won't get that taste right? So, it is okay to be called tamarind-candy as it is the main ingredient*," the old lady had convinced him. Recalling the conversation, he savoured the candy until the stick was dry. By that time, his mother called him to have something to eat and go to sleep. He did not want to eat anything after the candy, and with grandma's body lying outside with so many people gathered, he did not feel like sleeping either. He joined the herd in the compound, sat near her face and kept looking at it with his chin resting on his palms. The gathering mourned the old lady until the morning, and when the sun rose, they carried it out and cremated.

8
Beginning of an End

The dreams drove her bizarre and insane, and in turn, she made the people around her bizarre and insane. She could not express what she dreamt, not that she ever tried. She could only blabber a few words in juxtaposition – which no one grasped, and after a while, her words jinxed into the murmurs of a mad-women which no one even cared to heed. Slowly, the dreams crept into her waking moments. She used to see things that others failed to, even when awake. Venga took her to different doctors. One said it was just due to unrest, and another said it was due to the shock of losing her son and it would pass. One more doctor tagged her state as schizophrenia, and another blamed it on ageing. Nonetheless, no one could cure her. After a persistent recommendation from Sarasu, a well-respected guardian lady from the village, Venga took her to a few *tantrics*. They tried to lash the devil out of her with all the herbs and whips they had. The water and herbs, under the spell, were provided to consume so that their presence in the body could chase the devil out. The herbs and liquids came out of her body well-digested sans the devil.

When his wife's belly started to look apparent, Venga shifted his focus from his mother to the mother-to-be. By that time, everyone was accustomed to Asobha's daily vagaries, and her frenzy was a common phenomenon that drew more apathy and less attention as days passed. After a while, as the sounds of her imagination and reality converged, she was ignored completely by the milieu. She had become to others what the Vaisaki's coin box had been to Vanka

– full of noise, but of no value. She was customarily fed thrice a day, even when protested and she was cleaned twice a day to keep the flies at bay. She secluded herself in a room and hardly ventured out. Thereon, her insanity knew no bounds except the walls of her room. There came a day when everyone at home was fed up with her noises and decided to find a way to bid off them. A small outdoor room with an outlet and a private bathroom was built in the corner of the backyard. Venga and Vanka lifted and shifted her to the newly built room, furnished with a single cot to lay her flat asleep. They could not stop her from acting insane, but they sure did find a way to stay deaf to her. The room, left behind by Asobha, was turned into a store-room where the year's ration of onions and potatoes, and perishables for the house from time to time, were stored, freeing up the corner of the main hall.

With Aruna pregnant and the men ignorant of the outdoor room, it fell on Arobha to serve the needs of her sister on a daily basis. Every time she visited outdoors, she could not do so without colliding with a few memories from their shared past. She had stayed with her sister for her entire life. She was the only one who was there all along. When they left their home upon marriage, her mother Lacchu was busy teaching them to retain the honour of their family, instead of asking them to look after each other. That didn't mean they were not tightly coupled. In the initial days, they always stood in support of each other – whenever someone was in trouble, with anyone in the house or from the village, except in the matters of their mother-in-law, whom they both feared and yearned to remain much obliged. They had, together, dreamt of becoming the next Vaisaki someday. Asobha got there quicker, and now it was she who was preparing to leave everyone quicker. The image of her was fading away, along with her. No one wanted to be with her, let alone be her.

Not all days had been bright between the sisters too. Especially after Venga's birth, Arobha grew apparently resentful and displayed her discord in the open. It was in this space that Asobha relaxed herself from making attempts to stop Venga from the clutches of the caring aunt and uncle. Venga, in the absence of the father, looked upon Vanka from the very beginning. Unlike Rama, he had a worrying mind. Out of worry, he adapted himself to indulge in anything that was nearly safe for him, despite right or wrong. With time, he learnt the art of camouflaging into the ways of his surroundings. Slowly, he became what he camouflaged. He learnt to obey and yet, stay shrewd. Rama was not obedient. He raised a lot of questions and rarely looked content with any answer. With time, his questions alone painted him as disobedient and mischievous. Vanka and Arobha were repelled by his nature from as early as they could. Asobha was no exception. But she bore him as she had to. Vaisaki was unlike others. In her experience of life, Rama was fun to live with. Also, a grandmother doesn't need an obedient grandkid. A playful and mischievous one was a boon to her.

When Asobha reminiscenced about her children's early days, all she could think of doing was to worry about. Having lost her husband at the prime of her life, she was engulfed by the ponderings over the prospect of remaining a widow for the rest of her life. She did not heed Vaisaki's advice or hints about getting remarried. Asobha rejected the topic of remarriage outright as Kubja's honour was sitting on her forehead, and remaining a widow was part of that contract. Every day her thoughts fought against the choices she made, and they left a wide gap between how she attended to her children and how she should have. Venga had a couple of lapses, but eventually, he fell into the trap of the surrounding system, filling the void of a missing father with the company of an uncle. Rama found a vigorous life in the warmth of his grandmother, despite the vivid traps in his surroundings.

Lying destitute in a dark room, she could not escape the torments of her own *karma*. Within days, she rejected movement and glued herself to the bed. The only movements in her were the bodily jitters and trembling lips which sometimes uttered the name 'Rama'. After sticking to the bed for a couple of months straight, the news of Aruna giving birth to a baby boy befell on her ears. The relatives and villagers, who started visiting the house to bless the baby and mother, also took a consolatory visit to Asobha's outdoor room. Anyway, her silence made it easy on the visiting people who had barely anything to say. For many, it seemed like their last visit to witnessing her alive. Some tried to pump the sweet news of her grandchild in her ears; some tried to console her out of Rama's death; some prayed to God for her *mukti* with whispers and prayers; and some just sat, glared and left. The people, who first visited the new mother, had a smile and stayed excited. And, upon entering the dying mother's room, would change their face to wear sorrow and sympathy. The contrast in the faces of the people was dominating in favour of the newborn baby – for every living thing favours another living thing, not the dying one.

9

Trees, Trance and Temples

The failures induced in his academic prowess made him more infamous, both at school and at home. No one heeded the aberration – how a kid who was excellent at academics and was scoring close to perfect scores a few years back, started to fail in almost all the subjects. For those who had driven his downfall, including his own family, his fate seemed inevitable all along, and it was a befitting logical conclusion! Others inferred that a kid who was judged immoral and dishonoured, who did not heed teachers, who could not care any less about the classes, who roamed around the village with no regard for time and discipline, was bound to fail. Eventually, though he had become what society had expected of him, he was yet an utter disappointment.

Venga left the village school and joined the town school to pursue studies in English medium. Rama continued his charade in the same school until the school ran out of the grades to teach. Vanka decided that spending on Rama's further schooling was money in the gutter. Others in the family did not protest. He was out of school; one less burden. Finally, he was left to the streets to learn. The apathy of the family came as a boon to Rama. He did not have to receive blistering thrashes from his uncle after every test and gosh, were there so many tests! The pouring complaints from the school took a grave halt. He was no longer compelled to the confines of the classroom. Above all, he had pockets full of time to attend to the tendencies of his life.

He churned his time into experiencing life away from the frictions of others. He made himself scarce to those people and those places where he was unwelcome, including and especially, the family. As he ventured through his teenage years, he learnt a lot of stuff on his own without seeking support – sometimes the easy way and sometimes the hard way. He learnt to ride the bike and swim in wells. He lifted the bike up whenever he fell down and ignored the wounds that bled. He made his own floating-log to learn swimming. He could travel to far-off places carefree and timeless. He could defend himself from any infliction of physical harm. And also, a few people from the village – those who had purged the past far into the corner – started growing acquainted with him, and they no longer hesitated to break the *buthhi* or share a laugh or two.

The fourteen days' exile in his childhood had acquainted him with the habit of keen sight upon even the smallest of things, in addition to the habit of spending long hours resting in the lap of trees. He had been climbing each and every tree and he had been observing each and every ecosystem in nature. Having met the *sage* on the lost path, it was tough to keep those traits from being instilled in every nerve of him. It was the same *sage* who had later ratted him out to the temple administration which led him back to his home.

✦

Fourteen days away from home at the age of eight could only be wild at best, bound only by the vagaries of nature. After crossing a couple of villages, he learnt to respond to anyone who asked for his identity with the answer: "*I am from the neighbouring village. I have come here to play.*" He was not entirely lying. He played with any crowd of kids – around his own age. He learnt several new games which he had not played until then or had not been allowed to play in his home place before. He was introduced to Gilli-danda, Tiger-and-goat puzzle, water-floating, swim-chasing, water hide-and-seek and many more. Not only was he introduced to new games, but he kept getting better at every game he learnt with the passing of villages.

And, he found enormous trees in every village he visited. Neem and Peepal trees stood at every deity of the villages and banyan trees in the outskirts. Many of them seemed to be standing for generations. He inquired with the locals about the estimated age of every large tree he neared, and in response, each person spit out a different number at random. Old folks narrated the stories behind some of the trees. They told him how someone's "*grandfather threw a seed on the side of the road. From the seed came the sapling, and from the sapling came the plant. And from there on, it has never looked down. It is shooting into the sky.*" And someone else would boast to him how his great-grandfather, who was the head of fifty surrounding villages at that time, summoned his workers to establish in each of those fifty villages at least one *ashwath-katte* – a duo of Peepal and Neem trees along with snake deities. In every village, he found at least one *ashwath-katte,* and at least one person whose grandfather or great-grandfather was the head of the surrounding fifty villages. Another person would explain how in the last seven generations of his family, every head of the village had been planting at least one peepal tree so that they always had the feed for the sheep and goats that their family shepherded through generations. The stories of the folks did not end with what was asked for. The stories extended to other smaller trees, and then plantations, and their crops and then to their life, to their family, to their fate, to whatever came to mind. He listened to anything that was narrated and for any duration of time. For a child who was away from home and missing grandma's epic narrations and spontaneous stories, the histories, personal sagas and the gossip of the village folk became a convenient alternative to serve his vicarious needs. Sometimes, he heard different stories about the same tree and the same story about different trees, and he heard different impressions of the same person and the same impression of different persons in the village. The experiences made him learn sensibly, keeping his beliefs at bay. Within days, he learnt to pass every village, and its stories, as if they were his own. After a few villages, he not only listened, he also narrated the stories he had heard from the villages he left behind. He recalled, a few weeks ago, he could only wait and watch for the bangle salesmen roaming across villages, or the palm-jaggery sellers who travelled all the way from Andhra, and several others who passed his village, with not just commodities to sell but also the stories to tell. Now he was a traveller himself. Though he did not carry any commodity to sell, he did carry a lot of stories from village to village. Sometimes, when he slept on trees for a nap, he dreamt of the rest of his life living like a traveller.

Upon reaching the great temple of Lord Rama at Ramapura, he came across the biggest banyan tree he had ever witnessed in his life standing in the middle of the temple, vastly spread around as if to defeat the sky's presence. After circumambulating the deity and finishing offering the prayer, he sat on the platform built around the temple for the customary seating. He noticed a *sadhu,* wrapped in a couple of saffron clothes, wearing a couple of rudrakshas around the neck and untidy hair all around the face. He had laid down sideways at the edge of the platform with his head resting on the support of his right forearm. Rama asked him if he knew how old the tree was. He answered that the tree had foregone the concept of age and was now as hard and old as a rock. Rama was intrigued by the answer. He asked further, "If it has foregone the concept of age, how can it be as old as a rock?" *The* sadhu explained to him that a rock's life lasts longer than any life that a human can sense, and hence he chose to compare the tree to the life of a rock to denote its state of virtual eternity. Rama was excited by the words of the sadhu and inquired his name. The sadhu asked him to call him by whatever name he liked. Rama was a little confused but not without intrigue, and asked him if he had a name given by his mother or grandmother. He nodded with a yes, without revealing what that name was. Heeding to the confused face of the kid, he clarified how the name others gave him was to aid 'them' in identifying and addressing him. It was not for him to identify himself with the name. And he explained how the names he had been given had gotten lost with those people who used them, and how he did not remember how many names he had been called so far. Rama had heard a lot of exciting things so far. But whatever this man was saying was turning into the most exciting words of his life, and he wanted to continue to listen to more of his words.

The sadhu, who initially thought the kid was from around Ramapura, realised that he was not from around when Rama followed him for a complete day, crossing at least four villages to the north. Finally, he called upon the kid to come close to him and asked him about his whereabouts. The kid tried to reply with the same answers he erstwhile used. But the sadhu wasn't asking him for the sake of asking. He really wanted to know. Upon asking more and more questions, Rama could not avoid revealing his complete story. The sadhu could not resist being intrigued by the kid's story, astonished by the happenings in it, and the age of the kid at which such things had to happen to him. All he said to the kid was, "In a way, you are fortunate to have the cruelty of life unveiled at this early age itself. Now, you can walk on the right path to see everything just the way it is. Everything will get clearer rather easily. Just don't ignore the obvious around you in the excitement of experiencing it or in the agony of running away from it." Rama could not comprehend his words. But as there was nothing in those words which intrigued him, he let them pass. The sadhu then asked the boy to return to his home, encouraging him to take the traveller profession in the later part of his life when he would grow old and big enough not just to experience the pleasantries of the journey, but also to defend against the adversaries along the way. Rama kept thinking about what adversaries could affront a freeman's journey, for he hadn't faced any of them so far. What he didn't know was that he had skirted them unknowingly. The boy kept following the sage.

The boy roamed as freely as the sadhu. They slept wherever they felt like and ate whatever fruit and vegetable they found. They bathed in sun, wind, mud and water. The sadhu taught him how to build a quintessential hut from the wood waste lying around, without having to break fresh wood. He taught him to light a fire. He attempted to teach him to swim once or twice, but the boy could learn only to flap his legs and stay afloat while holding onto something at the edge of the stream. However, he did learn to find the sweet spots of the streams to get in and out safely. He also learnt to climb to any branch of a tree without the risk of falling. The sadhu taught him about the edible plants which the boy erstwhile thought to be weed and waste, and he also taught him how to extract the edible parts from those plants.

That morning, the sadhu and Rama took a dip in the stream on the bank on which they had slept the previous night. The sadhu went back to the tree on the bank where they had built a small hut with the dry sticks and hay they had found around. He sat cross-legged on a boulder near the tree in *padmasana* for his *dhyana*. Rama stayed playing in the stream for a while. The water streamed along the length of the meadow like the necklace across the neck of the goddess. The pebble he grabbed was shinier than the water. He swung it to hit the stem of a tree a few yards away to quench his target practice. The pebble chopped the bark off the stem where he intended. A memory from his past hit the mind with the same force. He was reminded of the hit-stone with which he was struck by Varna, some time ago. The stem started bleeding, not as bloodily, but just enough to remind him how his nose bled at the time. For a while, the twists and turns that changed the course of his life, and the experience he went through due to the people around him, flew in his mind like the stream in the meadow. Beginning with Varna's incident, he slowly delved into how he had spoken to Vaidhe for the first time, and then the school days with her, and then that day which started his downfall, and the days which followed and forth. He saw himself being a mere spectator of his own life all along. He also saw how his experience of life in the last few days had been far-reaching and far more excellent than the rest of his life combined. Being in the abode of nature, he started to realise how he may never wish to return to his home. Just then, the sadhu, who had woken up from his meditation, called him from a distance, asking him to wrap up the water dipping and to come out of it fast as they had to keep moving. The boy, waking up from his flow of thoughts, finished dipping and stepped out of the stream.

As they pranced towards a village, for the first time in their journey, the sadhu handed a cloth-sack to the boy and asked him to hang it around his neck. He told him to collect food from the villagers as alms in the sack bag. The boy did not understand why he had to do it. Moreover, he thought it was a crime to beg, according to his family's honorary customs. In the words of his mother, *everyone in the family was supposed to be always on the giving end, never on the receiving end of the alms*. She had slowly inculcated that into Shunka's family. It was her most precious custom she had brought from her great *Vengadi* family and had imparted into Vanka's. If Rama was to beg, '*what if it was to go into the notice of my family?*' He failed to even contemplate the repercussions. The thought of breaking his family's custom paused him for a while. When the sadhu patted his shoulders, the boy expressed his hesitation and the reason for the same. The sadhu took him aside and sat with him on a pile of granite rocks which were laid down for the construction of a cow-shelter at the entrance of the village. The boy asked the sadhu, "What is the need to beg when we can find so many things to eat in nature?" The sadhu asked if he wanted to know why one should beg for food or why one should eat by begging. Failing to find the distinction in the sadhu's question, the boy replied that he wanted to know both, thinking that that way he could get his answer in either of the responses.

"When you request for food as alms, first you bow down to the food, not the giver, for food is more divine than any home or any person offering it. People can lock up the grains and other food items in their homes and cook and eat privately. But, they don't own the life that the food can bestow. They can meddle with food, but can never dictate the life-giving aspect of any food. Also, anyone who grows food is only caretaking. The life in it is of *Shiva's* work. How can anyone own something which was never theirs from the making to the breaking? So, it is not denigrating if you are bowing down to the creator in it. And then, you bow down to the quality of giving in the person. Again, *Shiva* in him," the sadhu ended with a smile. The boy listened with intent to comprehend the bits of it and was engrossed completely. He listened, wondering about the aspect of making something that was the most demeaning thing in the eyes of his family, sound like such a divine thing. The sadhu continued his conversation using as simple words as possible, narrating as well as he could.

He continued, "And about eating the begged food, you can just eat it as you have already begged for it anyway and your body needs some food to sustain itself." The boy laughed with the sadhu. "I can tell you more about sensing the life of others through the food offered in the form of alms, but it is not your age yet to experience it. If you are to meet me after a decade with the same zest you have for life now, I will help you experience it. But for now, if you wish to go and beg, look into the eyes of the giver and acknowledge." He finished his sermon and the boy, with half the clarity and half the hunger, proceeded to beg for food at every discovered door of an undiscovered village. Wherever the boy went, he called out the people for alms with the Sanskrit words the sadhu had mouthed, "*bhavati bhikshandehi*".

Subsisting on nature's alms and the begged food, both the boy and the sadhu reached the Avali exactly at the time of the great *Avaleshwara* procession. The boy asked the sadhu for the name of the village like he had been asking whenever they entered any village enroute. When he replied 'Avali', the boy asked for its meaning. The sadhu replied 'twins'. The boy asked why the village was called twins. The sadhu narrated the story of Avali.

"Long back, there were two villages, looking like twins from atop the hill where the *Avaleshwara* temple currently stands. It is said that the villages suffered due to the envious rivalry of two whimsical women and their families, one from each village, bestowed with affluence and abundance. In the display of their fanciful prowess against one another, villages came to suffer a lot at the hands of their families. And, people went into deep poverty and apathy. The people came to hear about a *rishi* from the Himalayas who was on his voyage around the world and was staying on the hill for a few days. They approached him with their prayers and requested him to relieve their villages from the clutches of the two families. The rishi, who had already walked across both the villages, took one of his disciples, *Mrila*, into the village for a reconnaissance. Along their walk, he talked about the people they witnessed, not just from those two villages, but from several villages around that place, in their state of despair. He made the disciple realise the need for settling there permanently, and to reform and enlighten all the people in the surrounding region. Both of them returned to the hill. The next time when the disciple, sans the beard, visited the village in a fitting kurta and dhoti, the two women couldn't resist noticing him. Their natural inclination to fight for the best in the material world made both the fathers of the women approach the disciple, and in turn, they approached the rishi. After a long conversation, the rishi made both the fathers see how it was in the best interest of everyone that both their daughters be married to his disciple. And, the fathers needed just a small talk with the already convinced duo. In a few days, the marriage of Mrila, with the women from the twin villages, was conducted with the grace of the rishi who left with the rest of his disciples immediately after the marriage. Later, Mrila had the twin villages turned into heavenly abodes within a year. It was an easy task once the vanity of the affluence was reined in and pulled towards a better cause. He bridged the two villages and called it Avali. It was only inevitable for what was happening in the twin villages to spread across the surrounding region. When the entire region was prosperous, they decided to build a temple in the name of the rishi who had blessed them. They approached Mrila to carry out the task. He suggested the top of the hill as the spot for the temple to which everyone consented. He supervised the temple building with the right *vaastu* and materials. When people asked him for the name of his guru to consecrate the deity, he asked them to establish a linga instead and offer prayers to *Eshwara*. With time, *Eshwara* of Avali became *Avaleshwara*."

Rama could only be fascinated by the tale of the village. The thought that such a hill was at a reachable distance tickled his senses. The sadhu realised it was the right time, and he asked Rama for the meaning of his village's name. The kid said that he did know the meaning and no one ever cared to explain. The sadhu said that there could be a similar story behind his village's name too and he would definitely narrate it if he knew the name. The kid was a little hesitant. But drawing confidence from the fact that they had travelled too far away from his village for the sadhu to take him all the way back, the boy revealed the name Bani to him. The sadhu narrated the meaning and story of the village which sounded interesting to the boy but not as exciting as Avali. By the end of Bani's story, they had already gone past Avali, climbed the summit of the hill and reached the temple. The sadhu took Rama to a vantage point to view the village. Rama could not find any twin-looking villages in the entire spread of sight beneath the sky. He saw one widespread cluster of houses. He turned to the sadhu in confusion. He, who grasped the confusion in Rama's look, explained to him how the tale was from a long time ago, and how, after Mrila's time, the two villages spread towards each other and around to become one. "If you can notice the stream passing through the centre of the village, that is what was separating the villages. There was one to its right. And the exact other one to the left. Now, they have merged – as inseparable as they can be," the sadhu clarified.

For a while, they sat quietly on a boulder at the vantage point. The sadhu broke the silence by asking about Rama's family and friends. He was not direct in asking this time. He eased into him by telling Rama that he could visit that beautiful place again and again with his family and friends. By the end of his inquiry, he could not extract a lot of information, but he knew enough to realise that the boy had a considerable family who could be looking for him. After resting at the view point for some time, they went into the temple to seek the grace of *Avaleshwara* and offer their prayers. After the prayers, they sat in the verandah of the inner temple for a while and then walked out. The sadhu took the boy into a small room where a couple of ladies sat across the tables on their chairs, writing something into large books, and one man was talking into a small mic. Whatever the man was saying was audible to Rama from the loudspeakers around. The sadhu asked Rama to wait outside for him. The boy went out and sat on the bench at the entrance of the room waiting. After a couple of minutes, the sadhu called for Rama with a loud voice. His voice was heard through the loudspeaker sounds, and the boy entered the room. He asked Rama to stay in the room for a while. He pointed a finger at a lady and told him that the lady would take care of him in his absence. The sadhu left the place. Rama was not totally comfortable with the lady's company. But the procession crowd in the temple, and the absence of a guardian, put him in an unsettling but obedient position.

In the next few minutes, like the unexpected thunder of a dark cloud on a spring day, an announcement was made in favour of a missing boy from Bani village. Rama attempted to escape upon hearing the announcement. He was captured by his guardian lady before his escape, and in a few minutes, a couple of men claiming to be from Bani visited the room asking for the boy. The lady asked the boy if he recognised the two men from his village. The boy nodded no with his reluctant head and dull eyes. Before the lady could ascertain the legitimacy of the claim made by the two men, a man claiming to be a police sub-inspector, who was in his civil dress, entered the room asking for 'Rama from Bani village'.

10
Caravan of Freedom

He had stopped raising any questions in the school. The last question he had raised in the school ever was when his English teacher came in and uttered the name of the chapter he was about to teach – *The King of Comedy,* a chapter on Charlie Chaplin. Being interested in the stories of kings and kingdoms from his childhood and being unaware of the meaning of *comedy*, he asked his teacher, "Sir, where is Comedy situated?" The boy, whose most stupid questions were answered with due consideration a few years back, was now retorted with satire and humiliation at every question. This time too, the teacher did not miss the chance to turn the meaning of *comedy* into a memory of utter humiliation for Rama. "Le, Rama, you stupid. Comedy is something to do with joking and laughing. It is not a place, you monkey!" The whole class burst into laughter. Most of his classmates, even those who had no idea of the word comedy, missed no chance to laugh at their teacher's comment. The more his peers turned their back on him, the more he turned his back on schooling. Every day, sitting in a corner of the classroom, he searched his curiosity elsewhere through the windows. The world kept calling him through the windows while he waited for the long bell to ring. When the bell dispersed him from the corner, he strode in a single breath to his house just to relieve the weight on his shoulders unto the corner of his room and he took an undirected walk across the village.

For a while, after Vaisaki's demise, there was no person with whom Rama had privy talks. Not that he had anything privy to speak with anyone for that matter. However, there were innumerable times when the incidents from Ramayana, Mahabharata and Puranas, which his grandmother narrated, came back whispering in his solace. At the same time, he vividly remembered the sadhu from his adventurous fortnight whenever he thought of a peculiar aspect of life, or when he came across something in his village life that was reminiscent of that fortnight. Sometimes he thought of his father who, from his grandmother's recollections, was the most attached person to baby Rama in that first year of his life. The thought of his grandmother, the sadhu and his demised father evoked only a smile on his face and nothing else, even at the worst crossroads of his life. While the reason which put a smile on his face varied with person, nothing brought distress to his mind, for he had learnt to live pleasantly regardless of whatever happened rather than hoping for something pleasant to happen.

The freedom of life had arrived. It started arriving with the apathy of his family. Later, when his school where he was bothersome turned inconsiderate of him. And then, Venga left his school when Rama was in the seventh grade. Amid his newly acquired freedom, Rama cared least about the indifference of his uncle and the outright differentiation displayed between his brother's and his education. While Venga was sent to a nearby town school to study in English medium, not with the prospect of better education, but to earn more respect in the eyes of the village, Rama could only take respite by the fact that he no longer had to listen to his brother complaining about the humiliations from his classmates and friends because of the percolated rumours about his perceived ignominious brother. With little effort about his education, from everyone around and himself, he was gradually ignored by others for his absence from the classroom, and eventually, the school. His uncle did not let go of the opportunity to play around with Rama's education towards further misfortune. At first, Vanka stopped paying the school fees when Rama started to fail the exams. Later, when Rama stopped entering the school upon being insisted by the school administration, in lieu of the due, the uncle found a chance to punish him further by banishing him from the interiors of an unwelcome home. By that time, the village had become more hospitable to the boy than his own home, and he roamed aloof around and across the village with ease and comfort. This was the time he befriended Ajjamma, a dear childhood friend of his grandmother. While his grandmother had settled alone in the eastern corner room of the house in her last days, Ajjamma had been spending her days in a monastery in the eastern corner of the village. She had dedicated her life to the service and teachings of the sage of Kyvar, whose name she worshipped in all her awareness, and in his name that she served people with all her kindness. She wasn't new to the affairs of Rama's family, or any family in the village for that matter. She had heard a lot about the affairs of Shunka's family directly from Vaisaki whenever they met for evening prayers or while snacking together on betel leaves and nuts. She vividly remembered the time Vaisaki named the boy Rama. Ajjamma had stood beside her and had tried to oracle his future to be as enlightened as Rama's. Now every time she saw him, and had been seeing him as a better-enlightened being than anyone else in the village, she remembered her oracle carefully and silently cursed herself for not bettering her blessing – for not blessing him happiness along with awareness, for not blessing him courage with tolerance, for not blessing him with the bare minimum support of a humane family until he set out on his own into the world and lived his life in full.

It was usual for Ajjamma to invite anyone who passed the monastery for a bowl of sour-rice, if ready-cooked or at least for a glass of lemon juice. However, when she saw Rama passing, something about his face boosted her kindness and she insisted he have a complete meal. She would cook a fresh ghee-pongal just for him, and she would offer a glass full of lemon juice at the end of the meal. If the plants which she had planted in the compound of that little monastery were kind enough to have borne vegetables, she would cook hot sambar with tender vegetables along with the boiled rice. She always went the extra mile to satiate Rama's hunger. She had heard about his hunger days as well as about his ostracised days from Vaisaki. Also, she had witnessed and was witnessing him vagabonding. In the final days of her life, when she was trying to wreck all the bondage of life and treat everyone's life with equity, she could not resist seeing her own demised grandchild beckoning in the eyes of Rama. It had been more than five years since she had lost her only grandson to the cruel play of fate. Sunil, had he been alive, would have grown as old and tall as Rama by now. Every time she served Rama her meal, and sat slanted against the wall as he ate, she could not resist taking a tour into a vivid dream of possible present times with her grandson – had he been alive. And every time, the dream would be interrupted by Rama asking for water to wash his hands. Sometimes Ajjamma would make small talk with him. But most of the time, immediately after the meals, Rama would try to vacate the place. Whenever he was in the presence of Ajjamma, she would remind him of her grandson. And Sunil would remind him of his mother's words. To stay away from that pressing thought, he avoided sticking to that place for long.

As he grew older, the family cared for him less, and the home moved farther from him. He had become nomadic, had found his job in roaming, and his food in nature or in the invited homes, and he often rested on any *ashwath-katte* or on the floor inside the temple compound. He seldom visited his house, and that too, when he was coerced by his mother on the days when they had relatives visiting and inquiring about him. With time, it became a conventional pact that the mother and the son had arrived at, without a formal negotiation. For his part in the pact, he was let to live his life according to his wish and she was happy that he was kept away from his uncle for as much time as possible.

For someone who was free from the hassles of the lousy milieu and had entered into the wilderness of nature, life was terrifyingly smooth. Though the entire village thought he was illiterate, he knew enough about the intricacies of the deadly nature and the dynamics of the rolling village which very few could even contemplate. He knew a lot about the seasonal trees; he knew which plant flowered when; he knew which tree bore fruit in which month; he knew when it was about to rain; he knew where the sheep herds went looking for green pastures at any given time; he knew where and when the snakes and mongooses would hide or appear, and he knew how to catch and release them with ease; he knew how to rest in any tree-shade without the fear of the crawlers and the creepers, also without the fear of a branch falling; he knew who farmed which crop during which season; he knew which branch to climb safely upon a tree; he knew which branch to be cleared to avoid a sudden fall along the road. The caravan of his freedom had taken him through the soul of his village into farther places elsewhere. Being a persistent nomad, he knew which temple was full of life, with a procession and the people, during which festival. He missed no chance to roam around the magnificent places on auspicious days. Every time he visited a crowded temple, he came back to his village with much fervour. He was known to pluck and distribute to his acquaintances some of the fruits which they had no idea could be found in the vicinity of their village. He did the same with several flowers and tender leaves of utility. In the beginning, he did all those things voluntarily. But as time went by, the villagers got into the habit of seeking things from him. They asked for specific wood and peculiar stones along with the fruits and the flowers. They also started asking him to bring *prasadam* from the temples that he visited at faraway places – where they could only dream of being. When he handed them *prasadam*, people would inquire him about the temple, the darshan, the surroundings, the crowd and the grandeur of the festival or the procession. He would narrate to them his journey and bring it alive in the minds of the audience with vivid details and specifics: the water level in the close by pond, a specific beastly sheep which was sacrificed and was fed to hundreds, a new tree in the backyard of a temple and the fragrance of its flowers which made it hard for him to leave the place, the stories he heard along his path and about the temple he visited. With time, as he visited more and more places and brought back more and more stories, people started calling him Radio Rama. It was the time the village had its first colour television, and the radio machines were slowly disappearing. But people couldn't get enough of the narratives he brought from his pilgrimages. Even Byrappa, who owned the colour television at his home, enjoyed Radio Rama's narrations more than any programme or a movie telecasted on his beautiful new television screen. Whenever Rama brought him *prasadam* from a tour, he would leave his vantage seat situated directly across the television and sit with Rama, outside in the verandah and have a chat with his stories from the pilgrimage. The visuals and the sounds from television would envy Rama's vivid stories.

From an avid storyseeker, Rama had turned into an avid storyteller. From childhood, he had been listening to his grandma's stories and watching movies on the black and white screen on the neighbour's television. He had also seen several drama acts on stage and a couple of movies on the silver screen, and mostly, he had heard a lot of stories – which he had heard – elsewhere and everywhere he travelled. It was only inevitable for the stories in his mind to come out, in their richness, as mind-boggling narrations. After a long time in his life, he was associated with something good in his life. And, for the first time in his life, he was known for something good in addition to the evergreen smile on his face. When the news of his storytelling prowess reached the boulevard of his street, and eventually the corners of his house, Venga couldn't resist condescending. "When one has no work to do, what else would he do other than sit and tell useless stories? It wasn't enough that he disgraced us in this village. Now, he is roaming around the world to bring more disgrace upon us. There is some saying right, '*for the one who has no spouse at home, streets are full of courtesans.*' That is his state now." He couldn't avoid despising the allure of Rama and also did not leave any chance to erupt repugnance against Rama from other members of the family, especially Vanka. "In a few years, Venga will attain marriage age. If we have to find a suitable match, we should prepare proper answers to give to the bride's family about Rama. They will surely inquire about his elder brother. We cannot marry Venga off without doing something about Rama. And, in his current state, we cannot even think of Rama's marriage. It is out of the question. You should do something, Sister. It is about your son's future. And it is about the future of the Shunka family." Vanka ended his talk by addressing Asobha. Asobha, clueless, bent her head, woke up and walked into the kitchen. Arobha sighed at the confused Venga and followed Asobha into the kitchen. She spoke to Asobha for a long stretch. There was some crying, some consoling. Arobha finally relieved her sister's mind from the conundrum. She gave her hope that if they could try across the land, they could find some girl to betroth to Rama. She spoke paraphrasing a line she had heard from Vaisaki a long back, "If you seek, you shall find heaven too. Is it difficult to find a bride for a crazy person?" Asobha was a little offended to hear her son being addressed as crazy, but she brushed aside Arobha's remark as she could see the reason in it. Arobha continued, "Let us make him work in the fields for the next year and then, immediately start looking for a bride. If he does some work for a living, he can be put off the streets and we may also have a better chance of finding a bride." Asobha concurred with her, and both of them got up to prepare food.

Meanwhile, Rama was manoeuvring through thorny bushes to pluck his favourite flower, whose name he could not know, and hence, he had himself named it after his grandmother, *Vaisaki*. The flower, when smelled, gave the odour of honey, and when suckled, gave the taste of elixir. Before he could reach any flowers, he was caught by the thorns in the bushes which tore his shirt here and there and made it difficult for him to pass through. Looking at his torn shirt, he came out of the bushes and cleaned up his clothes and the scratches. He thought of coming back later with a stick and a sickle. He walked back into the village, passing via the monastery of the sage of *Kyvar*. Ajjamma saw Rama in a torn shirt and called him to inquire. They sat in the verandah of the monastery under the shade of the canopy which was laid up with coconut palms and had dried. Their conversation went from the torn shirt to his storytelling prowess which Ajjamma had come to know through the village folk. She asked him if he had ever visited Kyvar in recent times, and when he nodded with a yes, she asked him to narrate a story or two of his visit. He hesitated for a little while. She broke the ice and asked why he was reluctant around her. All she tried to be was kind and caring. But he used to slip away from her sight as soon as he could. It was not that he was frightened or intimidated by her. But, she could see that his hesitation had a bit of a melancholy in its hay. After insisting for a while, he revealed that every time he saw her, she reminded him of her grandson. She became emotional and felt like crying. But, she took a deep breath and consoled Rama instead. "It is not your fault he died. You were nowhere near him. His mother should have been more careful. Don't take it on you. You are a good person," she said, thinking that he was feeling remorse for some kind of imagined involvement in Sunil's death. Rama replied, "No, not like that. When I think back now, I know I could not have done anything. But, a month after his death, my mother had told me that I should have died instead of him. Whenever I see you, I remember Sunil. Whenever I remember him, I recall my mother's words without any effort." Ajjamma did not know what to say. And, the knowledge that Asobha could say something like that to her son came as a surprise to her. She couldn't fathom the plight of that boy. The silence prolonged the evening with Sunil in the ponderings of both their minds.

11
Play of Death

After the midterm exams, after all that mind-scratching studying and the life-numbing nightly tuitions, the Dussehra holidays had come as a befitting reply of life to schooling. The first of a month-long holiday and a month-long festivity. Sunil was woken up by his mother, Saroja, at six in the morning. She took away the sheets from him. Slapping on his buttocks, she asked him to remove the clothes in which he had peed in while asleep. He woke up, sat down on the mat, rubbed his eyes and pleaded for breakfast. "Breakfast at six? What is this new habit? Change your clothes, wash your mouth and come. I will boil a glass of milk by then," Saroja replied. Once she served him the milk, she asked her mother-in-law, Ajjamma, to prepare breakfast early for Sunil and she packed a load of laundry along with the brush and detergents. She unloaded some clothes onto a cotton dhoti, wrapped it into a lump, put the lump on her head, held a couple of buckets in her hand, and stepped out of the house. Seeing his mother leave, Sunil came running outside and demanded breakfast again, rubbing his stomach in hunger. She said that his grandma would prepare the food in a short time and he could eat then. As she moved away a few metres, Sunil ran to his mother and said he would accompany her. "What would an eight-year-old do with the laundry?" Moreover, as she was going alone, she could not keep him occupied while washing clothes. She insisted that he returned home and to that effect, shouted to her mother-in-law to take him back home. By the time Ajjamma reached him, he started crying and kept his stubborn act up. Seeing his tears,

Ajjamma nudged her to take him along. Saroja was hesitant. She had to finish the clothes before the sun brightened fully and later, she had to accompany her husband in the farm work. The weed had outgrown the crop and she was tasked to clear the weed in the entire acre by the end of the day. Her husband, Narappa, had already been to the fields to start spraying the pesticides and he was supposed to go to the nearby town to buy jute thread – to tie the plants, and threaded-valves – for the water-pipes' repair work. If she happened to take her son, he would definitely slow her down a lot with his mischief. She was in a dilemma. That was when she saw Asobha and Arobha walking along the street in the company of Rama and Venga. They had their portion of laundry on their heads and their portion of kids at their hands. Saroja asked them, "Where are you going to wash?" "We are going near Bhadrappa's water tank," Arobha replied. Saroja joined them along with Sunil. Ajjamma shouted to Sunil that she would have prepared his favourite *ghee-pongal* by the time they returned, and she bid goodbye to her grandson and walked back home.

Bhadrappa's tank was one of its kind in the village. To the village which had seen only the wells and borewells, Bhadrappa's water tank, built of rock and concrete, seemed like a place of ease and convenience in many ways for many chores. It had become a preferred place for laundry by several housewives, but it was usually frowned upon by the owner. When the three ladies reached the tank, Bhadrappa was still near the tank. He had come early in the morning to switch on the borewell motor to let the tank fill. A five-inch pipe in a corner was vigorously pumping water into the tank with a roaring thud, falling down from a few feet. The force of the falling water, along with the motor noise, rendered the close by voices feeble and the ripples caused by the fall had pushed the layer of green algae on the water to the opposite half of the tank. One side of the tank, towards the muddy road, was lined with coconut trees and it was only obvious for its ferns and dried coconuts to be floating along the surface of the water in consonance with the algae. The dried leaves willfully fell into the tank, bidding goodbye to the Indian pigeon trees and mango trees, surrounding the other sides of the tank. When the tank was still, the bottom of the tank could be seen at some spots. But when the water was filling from the pipe, the froth caused by the thudding of the falling water blocked one half of the tank from exposing its slippery bottom, filled with rock pellets, small crabs, fishes and tadpoles, being reared along with a couple of tortoises. The other half of the tank was rendered opaque by the algae and the dry matter. The three ladies sat near the water pipe, arranging their laundry and buckets on the stones laid specially for washing clothes. Bhadrappa, having noticed people using his tank water for laundry and dirtying it with detergents and stain dirt, had built a special place on the bank of the tank a few feet away from the main outlet. He had also arranged for a separate one-and-a-half-inch tap to vent out water from the bigger pipe to aid the women in accessing water with ease and staying away from the water in the tank. While the women unwrapped their dhoti full of clothes and prepared to rinse them, Bhadrappa arrived at the tank and asked the women not to dirt the tank water. The women, pointing at the layer of green algae, mocked him asking how they could dirty the tank anymore. As Bhadrappa was leaving, the kids tried to play at the tap which was supposed to fill the buckets, and started their game of mischief early. Asobha shouted at them and asked them to get down from the embankment of the tank and play somewhere close by. As they moved along the line of coconut trees, Saroja shouted at them, asking them to stay away from the coconut trees as she noticed a lot of dried ferns and coconuts on the trees. Intimidated by the ladies and in an attempt to be free from further tantrums, the kids found an open space on the opposite side of the tank where the water was let out to the fields downstream.

At the opening of the tank into the downstream canal, water staggered around and within the confines of a few small pots of mud-locked water, the tadpoles were nesting and sprinting with all the life they had. The kids found a perfect place to spend their time by playing catch-and-release of the tadpoles. The game was to attempt to catch as many tadpoles in a single grasp of their welled palms, and release them later and then repeat the same. The game was played in rounds of three. The best of three was considered for victory. Every time, Sunil won with his reckless grabbing of as many tadpoles as possible, even if it meant grabbing a portion of dirt from underneath. Rama tried the trick of forming a net using his palms and slowly moving them underneath the sprinting tadpoles. But, every time, he was surprised by their agility. Venga was nowhere close in the game, and his frustration was also the reason that the three guys had to quit their play with the tadpoles and move further away in search of new avenues to squander the time. They saw the Indian pigeon tree and lingered for the pink fruit. The kids tried to quickly grab the fallen fruit and pluck the low-hanging bunch. When it wasn't enough, Sunil attempted to climb the tree. But he did not realise that Arobha, from the embankment of the tank, caught the sight of him on the tree. As she got busy informing Saroja about him, he quickly slid down like a dropping fruit. Saroja turned around and as she did not see him on the tree anymore, she let them be with a feeble warning. The warning was unheard in the midst of the water thudding onto the surface of the tank from the pipe. But, the kids got the gist of her look. They further moved away from the tank to an open space, beside which the land was neatly ploughed and the lines were orderly laid for irrigation, and saplings were planted. Seeing the lines, Venga was intrigued. He wanted to lay down the blueprint of the farming fields in a smaller plot in the open field where they had arrived. The three of them discussed for a minute, created a game and got onto the business. They went in search of rigid sticks and tough stones to mark the territory and start ploughing the miniature field. Halfway through ploughing, Rama went and fetched several blades of grass. They turned each blade of grass into a miniature sapling and started planting them along the readied lines of a well-ploughed miniature plot. Venga told Sunil that he would take charge of his work and asked him to go fetch the water for the irrigation.

Sunil went out to find the right artefact to fetch the water. Initially, he found a few broken coconut shells nearby. He picked a couple of the shells with no holes and fetched water from the pots where they played with the tadpoles earlier. When he went back to their miniature field and poured the shells of water, it went unaccounted for. That was when Venga gave the idea of building a miniature water tank like the one they saw in the corner of the real fields. He started digging mud for the boundary on the lower side of their miniature ground. Rama asked him to build it on the other side where the terrain was high so that water would easily flow when they opened an outlet. Venga and Sunil concurred. When the tank was almost ready, Venga asked Sunil to go and bring as much water as possible, and hence he went in search of a bigger artefact which could aid in fetching much more water than a coconut shell. He found a plastic cover hiding half-buried in the soil nearby. He plucked it out and checked for holes, if any. After affirming its sanctity, he reached the canal at the tank's outlet only to find it was impossible to fill the plastic cover from such small pot-holes. So, he looked up to the tank itself. He climbed up onto the embankment. Choosing the closest corner, opposite to the one where the ladies were seated, he bent down into the tank on one side, with the handles of the cover in his right hand, and his left hand holding the top of the tank wall on the other side of the corner in support of him. With the tank just over half filled, and given his short hands, he could only brush away the algae layer on top of the water with the bottom of the plastic cover. In an attempt to reach deeper into the tank, he lied upside down with his legs on the bank of the tank, and let as much of his body as he could into the tank, reaching for the water and still holding the wall of the tank with the left hand's fingers. He finally reached the surface of the water and let go of one handle of the cover, filling the cover with water by gradually brushing, left and right and immersing the cover into the water. When the cover was full, he lifted it at once. The handle of the cover he was holding broke to the weight of the water and the dirt in it. In an attempt to save his hold on the cover, Sunil released the crucial balance he had through the left hand's fingers. He lost the support of the wall and toppled into the water. Having no knowledge of swimming, the fear covered his head and he flip-flopped in vain. The sound of his fall and the flapping of the water were nullified by the roar of the falling pipe-water and the shrill of the running motor. When Sunil had given up and sunk deep into the water, Saroja heard a big thud and turned around. She saw a coconut branch which had just fallen into the tank on the other end of the tank which had caused heavy ripples. She ignored it and continued her chore. With the ripples, the water slowly carried Sunil to her side under the guise of floating dirt. After reaching half the distance, the opposing ripples caused by the falling water did not let him pass further easily. The ripples pushed him to an edge at first. And then, the water returning, after hitting the walls, dragged him deeper inside, like the sea water drags the mud underneath on its way back. Slowly, he reached the epicentre of the falling water and he got muddled in the fury of it. In a few seconds, he rose to the top along with the water bubbles which frothed to the surface. Still heavy, the body couldn't float entirely. But, his shirt was light and soft enough to consume froth and stay afloat. The rippling pushed him again back to the immediate wall. Arobha, who had just stood to get her bucket filled with water near the tap, got a peek into the tank and saw the floating cloth. She was sure that she had seen Sunil wearing such a chequered shirt designed in red and white and pointed Saroja to the shirt asking if Sunil had two shirts in the same design. Slightly confused, Saroja looked around for Sunil to check if he was playing in bare body, losing his shirt to the water. She couldn't find him. At a distance, she could see Rama and Venga playing. With a little confusion and slight worry, she bent down closely at the floating shirt among the white froth and tried to pull it up. The weight she applied to lift the shirt was feeble to lift a body, but it was enough to lift Sunil's head above the froth and startle her. The shirt slipped from her hands and the body fell back into the water. She was taken aback in shock. And in hell-bent pain, she screamed with all her might and then fainted.

A farmer working in the nearby field came running towards the tank hearing the hue and cry of the sisters. The brothers left their play and rushed towards their mothers' voices. Arobha saw the floating body moving away from the reach. Picking the long stick she found beside the tank, she tried to stop and pull the body with the stick. She could not pull it off. By the time the farmer reached on to the bank of the tank, Arobha pointed him to the body informing him that it was Saroja's son. He immediately dived into the tank and brought the body onto the bank. Saroja was still lying, fainted on the ground and was dreaming a horrible dream. The farmer tried to resurrect the kid but in vain. Rama and Venga stood on the bank in disbelief. When Asobha saw her kids witnessing the death, she asked them to leave the bank and stand a little far away. The kids obliged. And then she tried to wake up Saroja. Saroja woke up to the cruel reality and her sobbing continued incessantly. When the farmer failed to resurrect the body, they took him to the village doctor. The sisters had to shoulder and drag Sunil's mother from the tank to the doctor's house. The doctor investigated the body and declared him dead. The sobbing of the mother rose to sky-high hearing the obvious from the doctor. The body was shifted to the house where the grandmother was ready with her cooked *ghee-pongal.* When she saw a crowd of people approaching her house, she came out of the house. Her sight vaguely saw a man approaching, holding in his arms something which looked like a tiny body. She saw two women partially shouldering and partially dragging another woman. As they approached closer and closer, her sight got better and better, and the picture became clearer and clearer. She slid along the wall in support and sat down where she stood.

Narappa was informed about his son while he was burning in the sun, sprinkling pesticides for the crop. Upon hearing the news, he dropped the pumpset and ran to his home in a single tread. The body was laid down on a wooden cot in the verandah. The mother and the grandmother were leaning in support of the wall while the tears dropped helplessly onto the dusty floor. In front of the entire crowd, Narappa dragged Saroja inside the house. Arguments were heard in the beginning where Narappa was questioning how his son ended up dead in a quick morning. Later, there was some response from Saroja, and then a couple of slaps were heard. Narappa came out and hugged his son in utter desolation. After a while, he stood up stone-hearted and prepared for his son's funeral pyre. Saroja came out of the house only when she smelled the incense. Coming out, she started shouting in an utter cry, "Ayyo, he said he was hungry. I took him before he ate. I could not even quell his hunger before his death. What kind of a mother am I? Put me on his pyre and burn me with him!" Her hue and cry reached the nooks and corners of the street. Ajjamma tried to console her. Having come out of the kitchen a while ago, she couldn't fail to notice that the aroma of her ghee-pongal was lost in the heavy air of the incense burning.

At the monastery, while Ajjamma was in deep contemplation, remembering what her life was like after the demise of her grandson, Rama was recalling her mother's words at Sunil's funeral, "No mother should witness her child's death." It was the same mother who wished he was dead instead of Sunil a month later. Ajjamma, coming out of her memories, saw Rama in deep thought. She interrupted his thoughts by asking if he thought about his grandmother anytime. He nodded with a yes. She wasn't convinced by his silent answer. She wanted to cheer him up. She asked him what the best thing was that he remembered about his grandmother. He said, "Tamarind-candy." Ajjamma went into the sanctum of the monastery and brought a tamarind-candy prepared by her and gave it to Rama. He took it with a smile and savoured it. She asked if he liked it. "It brought my grandmother closer to my soul," he replied. The conversation continued further for a while and took a sudden halt when Rama asked if Ajjamma remembered anything about his father. Ajjamma asked if his mother or grandmother had told him anything already. He replied that her grandmother had spoken about him in bits and pieces but his mother never mentioned anything ever. Ajjamma started painting her picture of Raju for his son Rama.

12
The Milieu of a Newborn

The father, who had been living in a titillating world, had woken up to the longing to be living with his newborn son. The initial few months were a little difficult for him as his care did not seem to be enough for the baby who cried in the absence of the mother every now and then. But it did not dampen his excitement. It only made him more possessive. No one was sure what had transformed Raju so much. In the village, he was known for his romantic nature to such an extent that people passed comments on him that he would flirt with even a pretty flower that he encountered. Vaisaki always thought he would hardly stick to a single woman and she was in constant fear of his possible ominous encounters with the women of the village. That had made her hunt for a suitable bride who came from a well-mannered and honoured family, who could keep him on a leash and at the same time keep him quenched of his thirst for romance. Asobha was the fifty-first girl whom Vaisaki visited in search of a bride. She was impressed with her behaviour in the first meeting. She was almost sure that Asobha would be the one to marry her elder son. But she was not hasty and stayed reticent. She went back home and started running a background check on Asobha's family. After verifying the glorious background of the Kubja Vengadi family, she succumbed to her desire. As if it was not enough, when she came to know about Arobha, the sister of her dream bride, her affinity to the Vengadi family doubled. Upon acquiring this new knowledge, she immediately sent out the message of her new wish of seeking both the daughters. If Byrappa, who was brokering the bride and groom visitations, could convince Vengappa to betroth both his daughters to her sons, she would be relieved of roaming around looking for another fifty to sixty potential brides for her younger son. Also, she didn't feel like she was compromising any of her requirements by seeking both sisters. When Vengappa heard the fresh news, he was on top of the world. He thought it was the best of all the fortunes that his family had had in a very long time. He didn't leave a chance to quote what was almost the motto of their family, "Fortune favours the honoured." And he bowed to the lineage of his forefathers and mothers.

Asobha was excited to see Raju for the first time during the first visit. When the match was extended to the second brother and the second sister, there was another visit for the sake of Arobha. After the visit, Arobha was not completely into Vanka, but the match was already fixed as if it had been made in heaven. Instead of confronting her father, she turned her disdain for her match into envy towards her sister and sister's match. Within a few weeks from then, the twin marriages were conducted on an auspicious day in the month of Shravana when the skies were full and Mother Earth was ripe and fertile. The marriage was organised in the Krishna temple of Bani village where energy was conducive and the space was accommodative. Also, its interior was well protected from both rain and mire. The temple was covered with the flowers of the autumn but the air was filled with the smell of pride of the Shunka and Vengadi families. The guests seemed to have visited to relay their greetings to the well-famed families rather than bless the new couples in the presence of the lord. The couples went home with whatever excitement they had left into their future life, and the Shunka and Vengadi families left the temple with the satisfaction of maintaining the dignity of their family honour in grandeur.

After finishing the initial customary house-entrance ceremony into the grooms' house, the night was to be spent at the brides' home. As the ox-carts would take a couple of hours to reach Katilu village, they finished the local ceremony early and left Bani much before the sun could think of setting. The new model of ox-carts, with rubber tyres, combined with *kaccha* roads, had surely reduced the commute time to the far away villages. When they started the journey, Vaisaki could not resist commenting on the changing infrastructure and machinery around her. "In our times, we used to leave early in the morning to travel this kind of distance. It took at least half a day and we often travelled with a packed lunch." A small girl who was on the cart with others asked why she had to visit such a far place in those days. Vaisaki replied, "Gattu village is close to Katilu. And the Gattu festival of Lord Venkateswara is famous in thousands of villages around. My father and uncle had taken me there for the festival a few times. At least we had wooden carts. Many people used to walk for days to arrive at the festival exactly on the immediate Saturday after the *Varamahalakshmi* festival." The conversation that started near Bani with the Gattu festival, took twists and turns just like the road they travelled. The stories were complemented by the sceneries that the dusking sun shone upon their eyes with grace. The tiredness of the travellers was quenched by the puffed-rice, packed in the cotton clothes, and the water carried in the muddy pots, placed well balanced on the hay-rings. The pots were refilled on the way wherever they found a serene and pristine pond. They reached Katilu before the village could light their lamps.

The herd of grooms' side arrived at Katilu during the hour of daylight as required. The rain God was kind enough to let the ceremony be hassle-free. The Vengadi family, as usual, carefully crafted the reception of their in-laws and their company with utmost honour and respect. Vaisaki was impressed by everyone and everything about that evening. The sugar mounds and the caramel-peanut lumps, in the plates of the offerings to the brides, would be feeling bitter at the sweetness of reception offered by the Vengadi family. On the next day, at her home in Bani for the brides' reception, Vaisaki upped the ante to surpass her in-laws' treatment from the previous night, as well as quenched her ego. The canopy of coconut branches was wider, the dinner was grander and the crowd was larger. The bigger crowd automatically drew bigger chaos. As both of her sons were made to sit on the seat for the customary rituals, she had sought the help of the neighbours and other close village folks. She did not seek any help from her birth-home, for the obvious reason of having had her husband humiliated in front of village folk in a petty fight. However, her brother was present at the function to register his presence. He left Bani later in the night, hardly spoken or even hardly noticed.

Village receptions were the best time for the women folk in the village as the function was solely run by them. All the women from the village gathered at the new couple's home for dinner, bringing their share of offerings – caramel-peanut lumps, coloured-sugar mounds, *chakli*, a bunch of bananas along with vermillion, turmeric, coconut, betel leaves and nuts. Each of the women, who stood as the embodiment of femininity, rubbed the turmeric and the vermillion on both the bride and the groom, blessed them by pouring turmeric-mixed-rice on their heads as the couple touched every elderly woman's feet to seek blessing, while the rest of them sung folk songs and laughed at the jokes cracked. The grooms prepared themselves to be strong-hearted to survive the day, both at the brides' and grooms' receptions. The women of either village prepared to gang up against the grooms to humiliate in matters of consummation and other privy things. The humiliation would involve all the sexual innuendos from the lives and experiences of all the gathered women. If some innuendo from the women backfired, it would only fire up the laughs. But if the groom tried something to counter the ladies and that backfired, he may be scarred for life. Most of the men either remained in silence or with an emasculated laugh, taking the brunt of the mass hysteria, or tried their luck with jokes and got backfired. The last time any man defended his respect amid such a situation was fifteen years ago, in Bhadrappa's marriage. He was such a funny man that even such a massive setting for women could not defeat his perfect sense of comedy. And in fact, he had ended up enjoying countering the comedy of the gathering more than they enjoyed their part.

The two grooms of the occasion were made to sit with their respective brides. The two couples were separated by a couple of feet. The women, approaching to bless, followed the order of grooms' seniority in their turn to bless. Few young ladies were blunt in putting forth their envy towards Raju's wife, to her face, in a comical way, while few others displayed it with a smug face. Some old women, who had daughters, joked about missing him out as their son-in-law, and some women joked about how they would have made him their son-in-law, had they had daughters. However, the women, upon reaching Vanka's pair, all they had to say was, "Vanka, you are a lucky man. You are blessed with a beautiful wife." It was not that Asobha was any less beautiful than Arobha. But the folk had nothing to say to the dull person that Vanka was, whose face had shrunken into lifelessness due to lack of any expression for the most part of his life. All that the village folk saw when they sat together was that Arobha looked more beautiful and livelier than Vanka. The comments of the village folk soothed Arobha in a way, but she could not resist envying Asobha while listening to the remarks made about Raju. Somewhere, she still carried the feeling that her sister got away with the better part of their marriage deal. On the other hand, Asobha's face was infuriated hearing the flirty comments made on her husband, while at the same time, as no one passed any comment on her beauty, directly or indirectly, as they did in the case of Arobha, she felt a little insecure too. She had to go through the entire reception function with both fury and insecurity battling on her face. As far as the grooms were concerned, one wasn't new to flirtations and the other was not heeding the comments anyway. For both, it was just another day, but requiring more tolerance on their part towards the rest, instead of the rest of the world towards them.

By the end of the function, the gathering had run out of songs to sing and the brides and grooms had run out of empty spots on their faces for the women to rub turmeric. The lamps were burning out the last drops of the oil for the night, and it was almost time to light the lamps in the bedrooms of the couples. It was the night of consummation. The brides went into their respective bedrooms with their respective grooms, carrying dented faces and minds from whatever happened during the reception function. It wasn't hard for Raju to undo the denting and consummate his marriage on the same night. However, Vanka had to sleep on the floor away from his wife. The skirmish which Arobha started with her complaint about the dull face that he had put up throughout the marriage ceremony, ended with her complaint about lesser grams of gold they received compared to her sister. Although Vanka tried to reason with her that it was customary to offer extra weight of ornaments for the elder bride, he could not turn the night breezy enough to soothe her. The bitterness was laid into the sex life of Vanka and Arobha on the very first night of togetherness. With such a start, it was only inevitable that Arobha's fury doubled three months later when she heard that Asobha was pregnant.

In the later months of her sons' marriage life, Vaisaki's farming fields were pouring the yield, whatever crops they sowed. She didn't hesitate a moment to attribute the credit to her newly arrived daughters-in-law. When most of the villages had lost their yield to the whimsical monsoon rains, Vaisaki's farmland was blessed with bountiful. Whenever anyone from the village congratulated her on the yield of the rainy season, she would say, "It's all because of the timing of my daughters-in-law's arrival." After the rainy crops, came the news of her grandchild. And then the winter crops. They had more than their share to celebrate on the coming *Sankranti*, the festival of harvest. She heard a few rumblings at home a few times, emanating from Vanka's room. The whispering voice of the disgruntled daughter-in-law did not hit her as a major concern at that time. She brushed away Arobha's rumblings and focussed on celebrating the confluence of treasures that was bestowed upon her family after a long time. The Sankranti was grand and she invited her daughter, Rupini and the son-in-law, Chandra. She gifted Rupini with a two-hundred-gram gold coin necklace and Chandra with a brand new Luna motorbike. This was long due. She was supposed to offer a minimum of hundred grams of gold and a bicycle while marrying Rupini to Chandra. But, her plans had not come to fruition as her crops had not yielded to her expectations. Because of the skipped promise, Rupini had to face a bickering marriage, and on occasions, she visited her mother's home and stayed back for a while to seek solace from the tainting in-laws and inattentive husband. Though Rupini's marriage was the first grand function in Vaisaki's life after her husband's death, it did not stay so for long. Now, with the coming of her daughters-in-law and with the newfound treasure, she was paving the way to a permanent solution to her daughter's marital bickering. When her daughter announced her pregnancy in the next few months after offering Luna and the gold, she thought it was a testament to the success of her plan. However, the repair of her daughter's marriage came at the cost of drawing the ire of her daughters-in-law who got only a pair of gold bangles, weighing around thirty grams. The opportunity that Vaisaki sought to rectify her daughter's life on the occasion had caused a bickering at her own house. Asobha, though sad, did not have much time to ponder on that detail as she was immersed in her pregnancy. For Arobha, it was a blister on the existing wound. As she wasn't brave enough to raise her voice on her mother-in-law, as usual, she rumbled at her husband in privy. No one ever knew that her repeated rumblings were what caused the walls of Vanka's room to shed the layer of limestone, faster than any other wall in the house.

When they first came into Shunka's family, both the daughters-in-law were involved equally in all the productivities of the house – from cooking to milking the cows. During the harvest, they equally participated in the farm work. When Asobha announced her pregnancy, Arobha took charge of most of the things. Vaisaki, with her ageing body, tried to lend her help in several tasks along with her sons, who started to help out in performing the household chores after a long time. However, the cooking was completely overtaken by Arobha and the transfer of traditional recipes of the house, which was conducted with both the daughters-in-law until then, started to fall into the hands of Arobha alone. It was a blessing in disguise for her as the people in the house were always respectful to the one who cooked for them. On the other hand, Asobha was kept away from all the activities and was given absolute freedom. Raju tried to exploit her freedom to the fullest. He started to excuse his farm activities to spend more time with his wife, not because she was pregnant, but because he knew she would be lonely in her bedroom. He started the habit of putting Vanka in charge of farm activities, and instead of cultivating the farm, he cultivated a habit of visiting home during the day on a regular basis. It was not that Vaisaki didn't know his intentions, but she did not want to stop him the way her husband had been stopped back in the day as soon as she announced her pregnancy, upon completion of the third month. Sex during pregnancy was considered an unfair treatment of the foetus, which would already have acquired a life. It was not banned, but severely frowned upon for the foetus to go through the consequences of the physical extremities of the sex. The husband was kept away from the vicinity of the wife's bedroom until the delivery of the baby and, then, a few months after the pregnancy for obvious reasons. However, Vaisaki didn't want to put her sons and daughters-in-law through the same customs for some reason. She allowed the couple to be together until the pregnancy became palpable to her eyes. So, even with her lenience, from about the sixth month of the pregnancy, he had to stay away from his wife.

The absence of intimacy reopened the old doors in Raju's life. Having been the most sought man in the village before his marriage, he had not lost his charm yet. In the absence of romance, the flirter in him came out with hardly any effort. It didn't mean he didn't care for his wife. He gave a slight leniency to the mischievous person in him. However, he kept his right hand incognizant of what he did with his left hand. But he couldn't avoid the coming-togetherness of the hands for too long. His slippery flirting gradually slipped into the conversations of the village folk. When Vaisaki inferred that her son was slipping from the arms of his wife, the fears from her past struck her nerves. She wanted to keep Asobha informed and aware of it. But she did not want anything ominous to be gutted into the ears and the stomach of a lady who was heavy on life with pregnancy. That made her hold the bitter worry for her daughter-in-law, and the bitter irksome towards her son, until the baby was born. The result of gutting out the truth after holding it for long was the blow to the head of the newborn, which was to change the facade of his life for once and all. The mother, at that time, could hardly contemplate the cruelty of the interaction between a tearless child, who had no idea he was supposed to cry at things, and the ruthless world, full of predilections. She could hardly contemplate that a blow to the infant's head, at the moment, had set unseen forces into play.

She could hardly contemplate that she was going to be enlightened in the barren grip of a deathbed, rather than in the cosy embrace of life.

৯✦৫

After the blow in the hospital, Rama had stopped crying. A week after that, in the absence of the child's cry, Asobha struggled to secrete and feed her child with breast milk. A week after that, her mammaries gave up completely and the cow in the backyard had to come to the rescue of the child. The visits to the doctor with complaints about the breast milk were not satisfactory for both the mother and the father. The doctor could prescribe pills for the pain in her chest, but the pain of a mother, who could not feed her child with her own breast milk, pierced into the nooks of her heart and manifested on her face every moment. To make things worse, once and then, Arobha intervened in her moments of dullness and spilled the venom that 'the baby must be demonic, that's why even God doesn't want you to feed him'. Though Vaisaki shut her mouth for spilling such a vile, it left a deep imprint on the mother, both in terms of her grief as well as her perception of the baby. But, in the fact that the baby never cried, she found respite. In the absence of the baby's cry, the mother relied on a timetable to feed him with cow's milk. While following the timings, she was unsure how many times she had missed his hunger without a clue. Gradually, with the aid of the grandmother, the mother learnt to pick up some signs of the infant that synchronised with his acceptance of the milk. On the other side, the baby which was devoid of tears started bringing laurels to its mother in caretaking. The gossip spread across the village and the family circles that Asobha was such a caretaking mother that the baby had never cried. To Raju, the gossip gave a feeling of pride in his wife. Only if the infant could talk!

For Raju, who spent most of his day farming and meeting people, the day became worthy only at the sight of his son. The husband, who was on the verge of breaking his fidelity, went on to become an obsessive father. Accustomed to the tender smile and scent, he started spending more time with the baby wrapped in his arms. He was revelling his life every day in the company of the infant. Excusing himself to spend more time with the boy, he slowly started delegating his tasks, one by one, to his brother. The mounding duties of the house on Vanka's shoulders, in a way, pleased Arobha who had always thought that her husband was a second-grade human in the house. Along with her pleasantness, she wanted to use that opportunity to hit another target. She started talking to the walls in the presence of Vaisaki, about how her husband was being burdened with more and more work, and how, in spite of that, she – as his wife – kept reaping the lesser benefits of the whole. Vaisaki understood the intention behind the rumblings, and she trembled with fear about the degree of disturbance that had crept into the house. She started giving more attention to Arobha from then on. She bought her an extra pair of bangles from the profits of the next yield in order to ward her off. Whatever she bought, the envious mind found no contentment as its envy was not served enough. Arobha's seeking for a child continued in parallel with the company of envy. Every time she saw Rama, she became even more envious. Every time she became envious, she yearned. Every time she yearned for a child, Vanka took her brunt. After some time, he couldn't take her brunt anymore. That is when he discussed with Vaisaki about what he was going through so far, since day one of marriage – from petty squabbles to long silences. Until then, Vaisaki assumed that Arobha's tantrums were one-off acts and mostly occurred when Arobha was not in the right mood. But, she now realised that Arobha was different as a person than what she had presumed her to be and that she was not right about the second daughter of Vengappa from the Vengadi family. She concluded then that she was hasty in her judgement about one sister based on another sister's character, and that she herself was whimsical in the garb of prestige while making her judgement. The possible scene from the future, where her second daughter-in-law would have marred her family for the worst, gave a jolt to Vaisaki.

No kind of jolt could impact the love of a grandmother towards her grandson. Vaisaki, without knowing, was competing against the love of a father, while Asobha was in a state of incompleteness. Sitting idle in a room for most of the day while attending to her son, her mind found time to wander. The head bang she gave to Rama at the hospital and her inability to feed him with her breast milk were hard to get out of the mind of a lady who had a perfect life planned. In addition to that, the rumblings of Arobha fell into her ears too. She was not as tough as Vaisaki. Her sister's behaviour put her further in the broil. Instead of relishing her boy, she was sobbing about everything else within. Raju attributed her changing moods to the effects of a post-delivery body's conditions. He was hoping she would become the person she had been before, sooner or later. It was in that half-person state that Asobha conceived another baby and delivered it after her husband's demise.

13
From The Mire, Flowered A Love!

Reminiscing the memories from the time prior to her husband's death, Asobha woke up from the floor and started walking towards the farm fields to refresh her mind. Her intention of the walk was defeated when three among the few people she crossed along the way asked her about her sons' marriage. She broke her walk halfway and started walking back home. The sun was setting, and her stomach was churning. A few months back, when people had been asking about her sons' marriage, she had thought people were really concerned. After a while, when she had come to know that they had been mocking her, she started feeling humiliated all at once, recalling every occurrence of those falsely concerned asks. Many in the village were sure that Rama would never get a match. With the elder sibling unmarried, everyone would question how she could seek a match for the younger boy. It was not like this matter had not wandered in Asobha's mind. It was just that the mockery had brought it into reality. Humiliation in any form was something that no one from the Vengadi family would tolerate. Her intolerance to the mockery pushed all her anger towards Rama. '*If he was like any other normal kid, I wouldn't have to listen to all this.*' Her mind spit out to itself all her perceived agony and readied her body to face Rama with might. He did not come home that night as he did most other nights. She waited impatiently till midnight. The restless mind could not stay awake all night. In the hang of thinking about what to say and what to do to Rama when she encountered him, she fell into slumber sometime past midnight.

She woke up a little later than usual. *'I can't wait anymore. If he is not coming home, I am going to him'* – the first thing she said to herself upon waking up. Finishing her morning ablutions, bath and prayer, she tried to step out in search of Rama. Arobha stopped her to eat something before going out. By the time she finished breakfast, she had entered *rahu-kala*. She waited impatiently. Like a predator which jumps at its prey at the right second, Asobha, who was standing at the door gazing at the wall clock, stepped out of the door at the second *rahu-kala* passed. It was already noon, and the sun was pressing on her head. Wrapping the brim of her saree around the head, she trod right to the usual spots of sheep-grazing fields of the village, where Rama was usually found spending his time lavishly in the company of herders. To her disappointment, he wasn't found with any of the herders. Her impatience to face him and eagerness to spit her mind out at him drove her to several other places. Finally, she found him.

He was found under the Indian Beech tree where he mostly played in his childhood; the tree which was closer to his life than any living person in the world. He was so attached to that tree that he had become part of its ecosystem. A new season had come collecting the toll for the surge of life it was offering. The dry leaves of the spring had surrendered to the breeze and laid bed under the tree. Every spring, occasionally, he slept on the bed of leaves at the end of his street where the blue kraits casually snuggled for a respite crawling out of the boiling earth. If some crawled under his legs and a few over him by themselves to find their resting place, he picked and dropped one or two of them to aid them in crossing him. He didn't mind the occasional biting of the ants and other insects either. It was unlike him to lay under the tree instead of climbing on top of it. That tree in the spring, which reminded him of his childhood like it was happening then and there, was an exception. After seeing Rama under the tree from a distance, Asobha approached the tree. As she approached, she saw a krait crawling towards sleeping Rama from the other side. She shrilled, at which the krait crawled back into the bush in a frenzy. Rama woke up to the shrill. Finding his tense mother, he asked what happened. She started ranting at him for lying down precariously in dangerous places and putting himself insanely close to death's arms. Rama as usual did not understand why she was ranting at first. "What if I had not been here in time and that snake had bitten you?" she asked. Rama understood why she was ranting. He replied to her that the kraits could be poisonous but not always dangerous. She was not ready to listen to his answers and hence, his words, as usual, went unheeded. She asked him to come home. He was reluctant. She turned to him and stressed that she wanted to say something important to him and that she didn't want to do it in the street like a barking dog. After her inconsiderate insistence, he followed her home. Upon reaching home, he saw her sitting on the concrete wall bench, apparently waiting for his arrival. He realised that she chose the outside place to sit so that she could dissuade him from entering the house. He entered the compound and sat against the wall bench. She bluntly asked him to get married. He nodded with a nay. She asked him why, and he simply nodded a nay again. She kept shooting questions in the form of tantrums. She asked if he was impotent, or if he had any affair with somebody, or if his intention for not marrying was to further humiliate the family. For anything she asked, he kept nodding nay with a light smile. Asobha, utterly outraged by his nodding, went in and brought out a matchbox and a five-litre bottle of kerosene. She poured the kerosene on herself and held the matchbox in her right hand's fingers signalling that she was ready to light and burn herself like the cooking wood. "When you were young, I burnt wood to feed you the food. Now, I will burn myself to feed your soul. I hope you will be satisfied with my death!" The neighbours, who were eavesdropping on the conversation, rushed out of their houses at once to catch a glimpse of the fire. No words came out of either of them for a few minutes.

Rama looked around at the people, turned to her mother and said with his casual smile, "You were always adamant and possessed with something about honour and pride. Don't you think what you are doing now is dishonouring and shameful?" Asobha replied, "What to do? For bearing a son like you, this is what I get to do. I must lose some pride now, to avoid greater shame later. You have put me in this vulnerable position. Don't forget that." Rama had thousands of words to say. But all he did was caving in with a bold laugh. He thought that was the better thing to do than belittling his own mother for her way of life. '*Do whatever you wish to do with my marriage. But this is the last thing I am doing for you going out of my way. Just remember that.*'

With all the jumbled thoughts in mind, he had crossed the village without his knowledge. His legs did the walking, and his head did the thinking, like they belonged to two different beings. The path led him instead of him leading the path. He had lost track of time but not the smile on his face. This was the most he had thought in a long time. The situation was not comfortable at all. His body could not stop walking in search of a cosy place to comfort itself. He lay down at the Hanuman temple where he had found a place to rest when he had been banished from his house for the first time, and the place had become his go-to place since then. As he closed his eyes, all the meddling thoughts vanished, and the sadhu flashed in front of his eyes from the time he was a kid.

"*Listen, son. If whatever you said to me is true, you seem to be not in the right company to live. My advice to you is to be very conscious and alert, especially around your family. I can't teach you everything about life at this age of yours. But consider this one thing seriously. If you are to have the same rapport with your family for the days to come, and when it is time for you to marry, do not marry. Avoid marriage. Your own family is prone to mistake you every now and then. For their mistakes, you are paying. If you are going to be part of another strange family, the equation of your life would be much worse. I know you will be capable of seeing everything, but you would hardly act on anything. So, heed to this warning and be wary!*"

The sadhu's advice came back to him without missing a word. Rama understood that in the spur of the moment he had surrendered to his mother's words and tears, without heeding to the sadhu's advice. With time to contemplate, he realised what he had done. The last part of the sadhu's words resonated again and again in his head, "*..., but you would hardly act on anything. So, heed to this warning* *and be wary*!" He turned to Hanuman, bowed to the deity and prayed without losing his smile, "Whatever may come, let me be."

Pushing his son into marriage, against his wish and will, seemed very easy compared to the mammoth task of finding a match for him. Not everyone in the world could be surrendered to by pouring a can of kerosene on one's body. Asobha spent several months talking to the elders of the village and the neighbouring villages, convincing them to look for a suitable bride for his elder son. Just by hearing her appeal, most of them turned their faces sceptical and without hiding their reluctance, they replied to give it a try. Asobha started getting frustrated. She was the one who wanted to not let his son be alone. Now, she was the one who started cursing him for putting her through such an ordeal, in the process of looking for his match.

After the marriage of Byrappa's daughter at her village reception where Rama and his family were separately invited by Byrappa, Asobha did not foresee his presence. She always thought he was never invited by any villager for any auspicious occasions. Being the mesmerising personal storyteller to Byrappa, Rama could not be avoided from being invited to his daughter's marriage functions. Rama had missed attending the *muhurtha*. Instead, he made sure that he attended the village reception on the same evening. The usual tumblers of edibles were laid on the floor. And as usual, the couples were seated on chairs near the wall, and they were being rubbed with vermillion and turmeric all over their faces. And as usual, the bride kept brushing off the extra vermillion and turmeric on her saree while worrying if the stains on the saree could be washed off, and the groom kept smiling to the audience while planning devious things to do deep in the night. The air was continuously filled with cheer, with the chatter of the crowd, and the chain of folk songs sung by the women folk. At that time, the singers were singing a song that resonated with the minds of every mother in the folk when it came to choosing the right husband for a daughter.

"Whom shall I betroth my daughter to?

Leave me a clue oh mother of all goddesses,

I will be in your debt for ages to come,
I will be in your debt for ages to come.
Whom shall I betroth my daughter to?
Should it be to a Vokkaliga who farms,
Toiling with sun and earth all day long?
That is where she shall be by his side!
Whom shall I betroth my daughter to?
Should it be to a Kammara who hearths,
Toiling with fire and metal all day long?
That is where she shall be by his side!
Whom shall I betroth my daughter to?
Should it be to a Kumbara who skims,
Toiling with mud and dirt all day long?
That is where she shall be by his side!
....

Whomsoever shall I betroth my daughter to,
Oh, mother of all goddesses,
Make him responsible for the family,
And bless my daughter to age well with him
And with the generations to come!"

Rama entered the scene at almost the end of the song. He was supposed to show his face to Byrappa for being considerate and inviting him, finish the evening dinner and leave the place. Subbakka, who noticed him while passing over the seated crowd, stopped singing the song and called his name on the mic, "Hey, Rama, come here." The noise broke the song and everyone started rumbling. One woman said, "Why call him now? This is a women's place to sing."

Another woman said, "Hey Subbi, he can only narrate stories, can't sing." Another woman said, "Not just singing, he can't do anything properly!" and laughed. The laugh resonated through the mic and reached every nook and corner.

"Hey, shut up. You and your ways!" She silenced them for the moment and turned to Rama, "What's up, Rama? Heard that your mother is searching for a bride? What is your story? Has it become difficult to be a vagabond alone? Do you need company to roam around?" The crowd burst into laughter again. Rama smiled at her comment, saluted her with a namaste and kept his focus on crossing the seated crowd without stepping on anyone. Rangamma, who was in the singing group, started the next satire. "People are reluctant to betroth their daughters even to those who are working. I don't know how your mother will find a girl for you. God bless her!" Subbakka tried to turn the satire around, "Hey Rangamma, you have two daughters. Why don't you let him marry one? You will get all the boons of the good deed - of helping a helpless woman in finding a daughter-in-law and a jobless man in finding a wife." The laughter continued but Rangamma escaped the conversation with "'*Get married, child*', '*offer me your daughter, uncle*'" adage.

By that time, Rama had also crossed the crowd and silently entered Byrappa's house and went to the backyard where Byrappa was busy looking after the dinner service. Byrappa threw a casual laugh at Rama and said, "You got jammed instead of my in-law. It's okay, come. Take a seat and eat well." Rama sat down and started tasting the first course of sweets at which point Byrappa came and stood against him to make conversation. "How is the food, Rama?" he asked. Rama tilted his head and raised his eyebrows in an attempt to express his liking for the large bite of *holige* he was chewing in his mouth. "Your mother was here earlier. She did not eat the second half of the items. She said she felt full and left abruptly." Byrappa informed. Rama stopped chewing immediately. He knew what would have happened. He realised what damage the loudspeakers had done to him. He then started minding the satires of the women folk. He could imagine the face of his mother when she must have first heard his name on the loudspeaker as she put a morsel of food in her mouth. He could see as if it was happening in front of him. He could see her face turning pale as the women humiliated him in the matters of marriage and the rest. He could see her mother leaving the dining table, not because she was full but because her ego was hurt. He could see a lot of things which he wished he could not see and would not be bothered with. But he did. He had come so far in life where some things were deeply chiselled into his life, and he could hardly fill the holes. However, he had learnt to live with them, and he wished others did too. One way or the other, something or the other came back to prick him again and again. He had already learnt to live with such a past that the pricks did not matter. He just wished everyone had a similar outlook on life, especially his family – so that they would live and let others live. He finished his dinner and washed his hands in the pool of thoughts. He bid goodbye to Byrappa and walked straight towards the Hanuman temple, involuntarily.

Asobha was fed up with waiting for him the next day. Her impatience drove her again to go in search of him. This time, she met him on her way. She grabbed hold of his hand and dragged him home. She took him inside the house and called out for both Venga and Vanka. When Venga came out and saw Rama, he started shouting at him. "Who let you inside the house? Get out!" Asobha informed him that it was she who dragged him in so that neighbours wouldn't hear their conversation. Venga calmed down. Asobha turned to Vanka and said, "Hey, Vanka, you take this guy to the fields from tomorrow. You let him farm and make him toil in the field."

Rama was still digesting the shouting he got from Venga. Before he could process Venga's words, her mother had already uttered her decision of what he should do thereafter. He lost his cool in that minute, but unable to lose his smile, he said to her mother smilingly, "You have no right to impose anything on me. You may be my incubator, but I am not your slave. And, definitely, this man, who thinks is my uncle, has no business with my life." His voice was so deep that it surprised every corner of the house, and he was so intense that his words were killing the dampened ambience of the forsaken walls. Angered by his audacity and irked by his unflinching smile, Vanka took a step to beat the crap out of both his audacity and smile. Asobha intervened. “You have promised me that you will get married. And for me to find you a bride, you should be working as a household in this revered family. I know you are easily fed as a vagabond, and you do whatever you like in the process. Marriages don’t work the way you wish. To portray you as an eligible groom, you need to follow me, word by word, until you get married. If you don’t keep your promise, you know what will happen.” She finished her message with a warning tone. “Okay, I will abide by your words until my promise is kept.” Those were the last words he spoke to his mother ever.

ꕥ✦ꕥ

The potato crop in the corner plot was completely looked after by Rama. The yield came out good. It did provide the family to feed itself for the season, and also to feed to the people from the village about Rama’s changed personality. Everyone in the village blessed Asobha that her days of sorrow were over and that she could rest in peace. As Rama started managing the work on the farmland, Venga jumped to take over Vanka’s responsibilities. He started travelling with Vanka to Chennai, Kolkata and Bangalore, wherever the yield was shipped to. At first, Vanka hesitated to involve Venga in his affairs, but he could not avoid it, especially after long insistence from both Arobha and Asobha. He had to teach Venga about the commerce and business aspects of farming. Being curious, Venga also learnt from his father-figure uncle about how to invest in land or how to finance the extra money et al. After a couple of months, Vanka had become dispensable at his work. However, he had the urge to be involved in what then had become Venga’s affairs. Especially the travelling part. Whenever Venga discussed going to the Chennai market with a load of potato sacks, Vanka insisted on joining him, to which Arobha would smilingly say, “Enough of your hard labour. Your son has outgrown you... It is time for you to spend more time with me!" Others would also smile with her, putting a stop to Vanka's insistence.

On a fine day, Asobha was visited by Sukha. His house was still close to Asobha's. But the distance between the two families had grown from the time of Rama's school incident with Vaidhe. Asobha was a little surprised by the visit of a long-forsaken face. The visitor, who entered the house with a gentle smile and a solemn salutation, keeping his ego outside the house, could not stop winning the bridled heart of Asobha. Most of the people visiting Asobha would have their conversations seated on the compound veranda. But she let Sukha inside with an unusual welcome and made him sit on the sofa in the hall, the place restricted to the people she thought worthy of. It was a way of acknowledging the dishonour meted out to his family by hers.

When the usual chit-chat was done, Sukha dived into the topic of his visit. "I am here to ask Rama for my niece Vaidhe." Asobha was confused. At first, she thought she heard it wrong. "What?" she asked. Sukha repeated the exact words with the same tone. After confirming she heard it right, she did not know how to respond to Sukha. The mixture of joy, confusion and worry was stirring in her stomach. "I am very glad that you have come seeking our relation. But I need to discuss this with my family. Let Venga and his uncle come back from the fields. I will talk to them. We shall meet later." Sukha exited with a smile and a salutation.

When Vanka came home and heard the news, he could not believe that Vaidhe's family came seeking their family, that too for Rama! He could not resist but to ask Asobha as to what had changed them. That was when Asobha also realised that her stirring mood at the time had made her forget to dig a little deeper into the matter. The family started speculating about the possible reasons. *Is it because she had also turned insane and dishonoured like Rama? Is it because they can't find a match for her after all these years? Is it because she likes Rama?* Arobha, who had been to her father's home, returned with a lot of souvenirs and edibles. Entering the house, she overheard the conversation and asked the group even before unloading the luggage from her shoulders, "Who are you talking about?" Venga woke up to help unload the luggage from over her head and shoulder. Asobha asked her to sit beside her and started to narrate the wonder she had to witness. Immediately after hearing about Vaidhe's proposal, Arobha asked, "Isn't she already married?" The family was flabbergasted.

ဢ✦ဣ

No third person knew that it was Vaidhe herself who had personally convinced her Uncle Sukha into attempting mediation of her marriage with Rama. She knew it was a long shot. But she had to try. It had been almost a year since she had lost her husband. She was not sure to feel relieved or sad. With his death, he had scarred her more than he had her scarred with his life.

After having to quit school in Bani and move away from her vacation place, Vaidhe was also made to move away from her birthplace, Maithalli. Her father, Jana, who was asked vulgar questions by a few of his village folk about her daughter, decided to move away from the place for a while to give time for the village to forget. It was a tough choice, given he had to be in the village every now and then to take care of farm work. He decided to manage his time from far away, as it would put a hefty pressure only on him. He thought it was still a small price to pay for his family's future and peace. Losing home and friends at that age was a big blow for both Vaidhe and Varna. However, they did not linger on it for long. The town of Klar had the power to fade away any scar. They found a cosy place in *Vidya Mandir*. They had more games to play with more friends. They came in touch with a lot of new things at such an early age which otherwise would have needed them to be an elder – had they been in the village. They met with a new discipline, new fashion, new play-toys, a new dialect of their own language which sounded just like the way they read in the books and new friends who had a different sense of comedy and mischief. Amid all those new things, whenever a boy came close to Vaidhe in camaraderie, she unconsciously pushed away. Her friendship with Rama, the guilt-tripped memory of him, had not yet settled in her mind. The lie she spread among her girlfriends in timidity, in order to escape the obvious humiliation – she reminisced on it every now and then. She wished if, by any chance, she could take back her kiss off his cheek. She really wished that the girl who saw Vaidhe kiss Rama, had kept her mouth shut. Wishing for an altered moment in the past, she subconsciously kept a distance from any boy who came close. It was not like she did not speak to any boy, but all her friends deemed to be called 'close' were girls. As time went by, she grew out to be the most sought-after and reliable darling in the class. The time gave way to new appearances on her body which led few of the teen eyes to pursue her friendship with more rigour. And it started to become more difficult for her to resist the boys, only this time they were behind her not just to be friendly. The more conserved she was, the more perversion she witnessed. A batch of perverts had divided the length of her commute road into equal parts to pursue her without competition. All of this did not happen much far from the sight of Varna who went to the same school. He felt suffocated at times when he was bullied by the senior boys about the matters of his sister. He did not have the girth to go face-off with them. Instead, he ventilated his anger towards the bullies by resenting his own sister.

The morning of Independence Day was a promising one, especially for those going to school. The town reverberated with the excitement of freedom on the day, including the schools. On such an occasion, when Vaidhe was walking on her usual road with her brother, competing about the wristbands they were wearing, the boy who was in charge of the Saint Mariya road dropped in front of her from nowhere and blocked her. After the exchange of initial perverse looks, he handed over a wristband to her that had a love-heart symbol on it and along with it was a letter. "Let me know what you think about it," he said. And then he slipped away from the place just the way he appeared. For Vaidhe and Varna, the parade of Independence Day started from there. Later at Lalbagh Garden Zone, Ranganna Circle Zone and Junior College Grounds Zone, distinctly designed wristbands, with the same-coloured love-heart, kept reaching her hand. And the letters – whose contents only the scribbler knew and the meaning of the writings which only God knew – kept reaching her trembling hands. Though all the wristbands and the letters found their place in the nearest dustbin, the discomfort found its place in Varna more than in Vaidhe. Vaidhe was in no mood to reveal all her everyday happenings in the home. But, for Varna, he had seen the threshold of his limited patience. As the one who ought to not bear any consequences, he narrated the parade of Independence Day to his father when he went back home after the day. Varna's words bore a tone of impending doom to Jana. As usual, he was worried and stuck in the vicious cycle of ominous pondering. He calculated the number of years since they had left their home village. After knowing the number, he thought he had given enough time for the village to forget about his daughter's old incident. He did not want to wait in the town for another humiliating story to befall upon his house. The plan he sketched at that moment stayed with him until Vaidhe finished her exams. Later, post her pre-college exams, he shifted the family back to his village. And he stopped Vaidhe from further education, and he made Varna commute by bus to the pre-college.

After being squashed by a surprise decision of her father, the dreams of Vaidhe had taken a toll. She started introspecting her fate which took a turn for no mistake of her. *'Is it Karma? Is it my payback time for what I did to Rama as a kid? Is it the same feeling that he would have felt when bearing the brunt of others' actions for no mistake of his?'* Many days passed in her mind without seeing the light. She never got the answers to the innumerable questions she asked herself. All she did was to think of Rama every now and then. Somehow, her mind evoked a desire to meet him with the reasoning of an unfinished apology. *'Can I go and meet him myself? Can I meet him in isolation? Is he married? Is he still in Bani? When I was a kid, I heard Uncle Sukha say something about Rama eloping from home. I could not overhear the complete conversation, though. Even if he is in Bani and even if I could meet him and even if I talked to him, will he respond?'* The mind kept bothering her with more and more questions without reciprocation. With so much time to spare in her life after the house chores and the fieldwork, she had no reason to stop herself from the beckoning of her unravelling mind. The unravelling had pushed her into the arms of his image which, with time, became inseparable from her mind. At such a time, her father came with an intention to marry her off. Something came to her mind, and she slowly crawled into her father's room after dinner with a plate of betel leaves and nuts. Serving her father a post-dinner snack, she brought forth the idea of searching for a groom in Bani where her mother Suneena hailed from. She hinted to him that that way she would be close to her uncle, and her father could respite from the fact that she was close to the family even after the marriage. Jana liked the idea. Placing his palm on her head, he said, "Sure, dear. I will start looking for a match in Bani." Hearing that, there was a glow in Vaidhe's eyes and a smile on her face which evaded her reasoning at first. She was about to go to her room and look back in wonder at what happened. She was going to question in her sleep as to why she wanted to find her husband from Bani where she had not been to in several years. The obvious image of Rama kept reflecting in her mind every time she tried to reason with herself and until the reason became obvious. However, after a few weeks when her father came home with a final match from a far village of Mangotta, her short-lived thoughts and whims collapsed like the pearls which fell from a broken necklace.

Being married to Valla was no boon. An alcoholic with no concern for a prospective family should rather be left alone. A pinch of cynical mind combined with an alcohol-filled body can do wonders in wreaking havoc in the life of the spouse. Even while inebriated, the bruises he imprinted every day on her body were carefully crafted to locate in the places hidden from others. The sex he had with her was as foul as his alcoholic breath and as forceful as their marriage. It did not take too long for her to associate him with the smell of brandy. And, it did not take long for her to get pregnant. She wished, 'if only nature had a way to stop the forced sex from impregnating women'. On the day she was nauseated by her pregnancy, her husband died of an electric accident. The man, who had half a bottle of brandy in his brain and another half in his hand, did not mind walking in the dark towards home. And, the darkness did not mind hiding the fallen electric wire on his path. The moment he stepped on it, all the violence he had thrown on everyone in his life passed through his body at once. He was unaware of the pain he had caused to others, only until he died of all the pain combined. He died with his body half burnt and half still burning. His pyre did not require much wood.

Jana, who had known her daughter's pain all along her marriage life but had been reluctant to bring her back home in the hope that her son-in-law would become a good person someday, now waited for no reason. A month after Valla's death, once everyone at his home had settled, he spoke to Vaidhe and after her consent, he took her back to his home to which no other person from her in-laws protested. It was back at her father's home that she revealed her pregnancy for the first time. Jana, who was already worried about the prospects of her daughter's remarriage, asked every woman from his relatives' circle to talk Vaidhe out of continuing with the pregnancy. It took a while, but he was successful. A few months into the pregnancy, Jana and Suneena took her to the town hospital and brought her back. On her way back with her empty womb, while crossing her alma mater, *Vidya Mandir*, the devious facts of her life started crawling into her mind. By the time she reached her home, she started realising how much she had let others influence her life. Whether it was her father, mother, brother any relative, a teacher or any acquaintance, everyone had tried to influence and manipulate her amenable mind, and most of them had succeeded in doing so. It was evident in the schools she attended, the people she befriended, the places she stayed and the person she married. The image of Rama passed her mind when she tried hard to recollect someone who had never tried to manipulate her. Thinking of him, she felt as easy as her breath and as comfortable as her clothes. The more she thought of Rama, the more she explored her own self. The more she thought of Rama, the more she regretted herself. She diverted herself in an attempt to evade the guilt. Her mind kept thinking about the new possibilities in the life ahead. She was hardening her mind and bracing her breath, in determination, for what was presumably going to be an erratic future.

Almost a year later, she heard about bride-search for Rama from the privy conversation between her father and mother. "Bani's Asobha is looking for a match for her elder son it seems. I heard the news from our village president," Jana said. The conversation continued with how Jana was shocked to hear that once a pervert boy, and later a vagabond until recently, had become a responsible man. Suneena turned her face into awe-struckness whenever Jana's face expressed awe. The conversation ended with Jana saying, "Let us see who will offer him their daughter!"

For the next few days, Vaidhe thought through, with her newly shaped mind and breath, and conceived the idea of attempting to marry the person who was always there in her thoughts wherever she went. After scrolling through several ideas, one stuck as plausible. She called her uncle in Bani and asked him to visit her during the festival of Ugadi. Upon his visit, she talked him into convincing her parents for a marriage proposal with Rama. Sukha was surprised initially. When Vaidhe explained to him the truth of her school incident, instead of thinking about Vaidhe's requests, he immediately started pitying Rama. Vaidhe explained how she had liked him from school days, and how she had tried to hint to her father about Rama by asking him to search for a groom in Bani before she was married off to Valla. After hearing all her utterances, Sukha said, "What and all have you revealed! Anyway, I will try my level best to convince your parents. But I am not sure if Asobha will accept a widow as her daughter-in-law." "I have an intuition that she will,", Vaidhe replied. Sukha tilted his head in submission to her words. Later, it did not take much time to convince Jana, given his concern for others' opinions and for the prospect of his daughter entering a house known for family honour and pride. In the month of Kartika, and in memory of Vaisaki, the first marriage after the last death took place in the Shunka family.

14
AN UNFINISHED STORY

Asobha had started to feel her hair giving up growing. She could feel her skin wrapping up and her body becoming rigid, day by day, hour by hour and minute by minute. Lying idle on the bamboo cot in a deserted room, she was frequently visited by Vaisaki and Rama. Rama uttered no word and stood in silence during every visit, just like he did since he last spoke to her before his marriage. On the other hand, Vaisaki refused to stay silent even on Asobha's insistence, just like she did even on her deathbed in the hospital when she whispered the deepest secret of her life. That secret inspired Asobha in an unintended way – only if Vaisaki held her breath until she revealed the moral of the story, Asobha would have received Vaisaki's revelation in the intended manner and for the good of all.

On the deathbed, when she called Asobha alone to say something, Vanka and Arobha thought she was revealing a secret of a treasure in her ears. It was the story of her life that she wanted Asobha to be aware of, as her elder daughter-in-law, so that no such incidents were repeated in her family, intentionally or unintended. It was the story that she had kept secluded in the corner of her mind.

When Shunka had been working in the gold mines several miles away and seldom visited her with his bountiful earnings, the home used to be filled with festivities. And in the deep nights of those festivities, he quenched his thirst in the company of his wife. By the next time he visited her, she would be carrying a baby in her belly. His mother and others made sure that the husband stayed away from all the carnal activities with the wife when she was pregnant. He had to stay thirsty until the delivery. He was patient during the first two deliveries. By the third pregnancy, he had outgrown his patience and modesty. The body, which took the brunt of dust and stone in the mines, could keep its integrity for only so long.

During the third pregnancy of his wife, he had become accustomed to staying away from the house. He started finding new companionship and ways to quell his whims. Not after long, one day when he visited the shop for a pack of beedis, Savi looked at him and giggled while handing him the pack. He asked what was so funny. She said, "I understand your pain. Poor boy. Six more months of hunger for you!" She giggled again. Shunka left the shop, curiously thinking if she used hunger as a euphemism for sex. He did not dig deep into her comments at the moment. But later, after visiting her shop several times, they had been into each other with sexual innuendos. Thereon, he was visiting her shop not just for beedis. Savi had been a widow for the past few months with no children. She had newly opened her shop in the corner of the village where the men wished to cross boundaries, in pursuit of debauchery. A few months into the third pregnancy of his wife, and after a few weeks of acquaintance with Savi, Shunka had started to visit Savi's home in privy. It was easy to sneak in and out of a house which was away from the village and was shadowed by lush bushes. However, nothing that happens in a village could be kept secret for long. His visits to Savi's house came to light during Vaisaki's fourth pregnancy.

When she was five months into her pregnancy, she overheard the conversation that her neighbours were giggling about. Initially, by the tone of their laughs, she thought she would hear a limerick or two. Little did she know they were making fun of her, regarding something that her husband was fooling her about. She didn't catch the name of the woman who was ripping off her family. It took a little digging to know the name and details of Shunka's companion in infidelity, but she wanted to confirm by witnessing him in the act rather than confronting him with gossip. She had already deduced that it was towards Savi's home that he crawled out into the night, every now and then. That night, when everyone was about to fall asleep, Shunka said to her mother as usual, "Ma, I am stepping out to check on the crops. Will be back late." He stepped out of the house with a torch that beamed him up towards his whimsies. Once he left, Vaisaki gave herself a little gap to grasp, and then she walked straight to Savi's house, sneaking through the rumbling bushes. The window was kept open for fresh air to enter, and it wasn't difficult for Vaisaki to witness what was about to happen with crystal clarity.

He jumped on Savi like a ravishing beast, locked her palms in his, held her laid thighs with his knees, and asked, "Is this how you dreamt?" He was referring to the narration of her dream from last night. She nodded yes with her devious eyes and an obnoxious smile. He lifted her up by the hip and then rubbed her cravings with his manhood. He whispered in her ears as he kept rubbing, "Is that mine?" She replied by rubbing back firmer. He grew harder. He sucked her lower lip with no lesser intention than to consume it. He was stopped by a strand of hair flowing from her forehead which got stuck in his lingering mouth. However, it was no hindrance to his inglorious passion. He swirled the blocking strand of hair around his tongue until it tightened and tinged her. When she moaned at the tinge, he asked her again, "Is this mine too?" His command in the voice, while asking for such minute details, made her so erotic that she bit his lips to the bleeding. So passionate was her bite that he ripped her undergarment and pierced her within a moment. She stopped biting his lips, not for respite but to scream with bliss. At that moment, when they were merged at their epicentre, their faces moved away to make space for their erotic cry. As the faces moved away, her hair from the forehead unswirled from his tongue, cutting it a bit. He then painted her in maroon with his tongue, from her face to bosom, as he kept knocking her up, held in the clutches of his arms. The act went on into the night until he was quenched. After witnessing enough to be outraged, Vaisaki evaded the place with an image of Shunka waking up and being surrendered in the arms of the concubine the next morning.

The next few days he stayed at home before returning to the mining work, Vaisaki tried to confine him to her house in the night with several tricks. However, Shunka had outgrown her wits, and nothing could stop him from pursuing his newfound desires. She stopped insisting on him after a certain attempt lest he would figure out that she knew about his affair and start pursuing it in the open. The picture of her husband's animalistic deed was hard to get away with. Yet, she did not even confront Savi for robbing her of a happy family. She was smarter than that. Vaisaki was more concerned about the future of her children. And she gave a deep thought into the importance of society around her in the life of growing kids. She could see the humiliation that she and her kids would have to go through in the future for the acts of her husband from the past. Finally, she made a decision that would keep Shunka's family reputation unslain, even if she had to sacrifice the half.

By the time Shunka returned home next time, she had kept a load of castor seeds powdered and safe in her cupboard. Every meal for the next few days, she made sure he was served with a fist full of castor powder mixed into it. To hide the smell and taste of the powder, she upped the spice content in his portion of food. The tongue, which was roughened by the hot air of mining tunnels, hardly felt the taste of anything other than chilli powder and salt. After a couple of days, he fell sick and stayed bedridden. The nausea and diarrhoea were just the beginning. The powder of love was killing him inside, part by part. The village doctor, who was called by him, brushed away the seriousness of his health as a common disease from his workplace. He provided him with a regular set of pills. In addition, the doctor asked Vaisaki to stay strong and look after the husband. Little did he know of her deviousness. A few days later, Shunka succumbed to the fatality of his ignorance and the brutality of his loved one. And a couple of months later, her fourth pregnancy delivered a deceased child. The residue of the powder had taken more toll than she intended.

With her in-laws' help, she managed to look after Raju, Vanka and Rupini. After the death of her in-laws, Vaisaki was put to the real test of life. With an acre of land and a lot of mouths to feed, she struggled to meet the ends. It did not take long to realise the brutality of life despite the morals that one adopts. In a few years, when Raju and Vanka were old enough, they started helping Vaisaki in the house and the farm work. Both the brothers and their mother tried to put Rupini into school at the cost of their labour. However, she did not find it in her to pursue education, and she casually stopped schooling in the middle. The time came for her daughter's marriage and then the sons'. And after that came the grandchildren. But looking deep into her life, she could hardly reconcile with the way she dealt with her husband. And often, she would ponder if she really went scot-free of her deed, or if the life that followed Shunka's death itself was her punishment. Being married at the age of fourteen, bearing three children by the time she was eighteen, murdering her husband and losing a child at birth at nineteen – pondering about her teen incidents, she tried to assign the blame on age, while trying to find respite in the thought that she would have handled the situation wholly differently, and with rather ease, if it had happened later in her life. But, whenever she thought of her husband, the fear of further tragedies in her family kept infiltrating her thoughts.

✦

Appearing in the barren outdoor room in her casual chequered saree and grinding betel nuts and leaves with her artificial teeth, Vaisaki finished narrating the moral of her unfinished story to Asobha. An unfinished story, which on the deathbed of Vaisakhi was juxtaposed with duty and honour, started to unveil the truth through the ghost of Vaisaki. The story was never about morality or authority. It was about the erratic nature of life. It was about the brutal reality of life. It was about not succumbing to the whims and fancies of life. The message was received late, but it put a real smile on Asobha's face after a long time. The conversations with Vaisaki, which sounded hallucinating to onlookers, had real meaning in Asobha's last days. So was her silent gaze at Rama, who frequently appeared along with Vaisaki, but always sat in a corner in silence. If her entire family life was weighed against the last few days of secluded life, the scale would easily tilt in solidarity with her solitude; so intense was her experience of life with the images of Vaisaki and Rama.

The images which initially appeared in their dying forms started morphing into shapes in different stages of their life. Sometimes, Vaisaki would appear from her midlife, shaping her in-laws with her love and knowledge. Sometimes she would appear in the shape of a new grandmother who just visited her first grandson at the hospital. Sometimes in the shape of a grandmother who sat down with her grandson narrating stories on the verandah of the house. The image of Rama also varied with Vaisaki's image. Sometimes a baby boy, a kid, and then his image of a teenager would go void in her eyes and then he would appear as a man and then as a husband. She was seeing the images as real as Rama had been seeing the characters from his grandmother's stories. Going forward, she started to notice minute details in their images. When she saw the image of Vaisaki sitting with Rama and narrating her stories from the epics, she would notice Rama's eyes shifting their focus point from Vaisaki's eyes to his imagination where the characters fell into his head in real-time. When she saw the image of Vaisaki passing the group of women while singing her praises, she would notice an unclenching grim on her face. She started noticing that in none of the appearances of Rama, she saw him dull or crying. She started realising that his evergreen smile was not of his arrogance or irky-trait, but the jewel he always wore. She started noticing that Vaisaki might have been worried but never had been angry for as long as she knew her. Asobha also started noticing that her mother-in-law never ever tried to impose anything on any of the family members – unlike herself, who had imposed a fair share of her predilections on every member of the family and had pushed a few lives to the edges, knowingly or unknowingly. Asobha started to wonder if it was the curse of Shunka's progeny to have in-laws from the Kubja family and to have the coming generations put through everlasting agony. That's when the image of Vaisaki came close to her ear and whispered, "Think not what you have done. Realise and execute what needs to be done, for the good of all, including the newborn."

15
Honour Gives and Takes Away!

The whispers of the ghosts rendered Asobha restless. To salt the agony, she started hearing loud noises from the other side of the house where she once ruled. She crawled out of her bed, held her support-stick as firmly as she could, and started walking shakily towards the backdoor of the house. As she walked into the house through the backdoor, she saw Arobha engaged in a war of words with a strange lady. The strange lady did not engage herself in the same harsh tone as Arobha's, but she was not silent either. Also, she sounded strange. She was speaking a different tongue. At first, she wondered why Arobha was caught in a fight with someone who doesn't even speak the same tongue. 'Perhaps, some misunderstanding,' she thought, and went to Aruna, who was standing behind the door, in the house, witnessing the skirmish along with their neighbour Sonna. With her feeble voice, she inquired Aruna about the fight; it seemed easier than attempting to interrupt Arobha who was rampant in her fighting.

Aruna, initially surprised to see her mother-in-law inside the house, explained what she had witnessed just before. She told Asobha how she opened the door to the knocking of a strange woman, who started uttering some gibberish words upon opening the door. Aruna had not understood any of her words, except Vanka's name in between, which was when Arobha came to the door. The confused ladies took the help of their neighbour Sonna, who was passing in front of their house, to decode the strange woman. Sonna, with his little knowledge of the Tamil language, tried to make sense of the strange lady, like he was arranging scrambled words. "She is claiming that she is Vanka's wife, and the boy hiding in her saree drape is her son born to Vanka," he said hesitantly, looking at Aruna, but crossing his eyes with Arobha now and then. His awkwardness while delegating the translation was evident both in his eyes and mumbling words. Hearing Sonna's words, Arobha sat down on the nearby bench in shock. A few seconds later, she came back to her senses and in utter outrage, she fell on the strange lady with full might, shouting slang words. The strange lady was not smooth either. Without even shaking from her standstill position, she threw her own tantrums at Arobha while defending herself from the impending fight. If Aruna had not held Arobha back, there would have been a do-or-die fight between the two wives.

When Asobha came to the scene and grasped the situation, she was aghast at first then started laughing at the twists and turns in the fate of her revered family. She softly asked Sonna to go and fetch Vanka, while Aruna kept blocking Arobha every now and then whenever the fight went out of control. Vanka came home before Aruna could give up intervening. Venga had followed him. Venga scolded Aruna for keeping the fight outside the house where everyone on the street and in the neighbourhood could witness it. He took the strange lady, along with her son, inside the house. Venga asked Aruna to prepare tea and asked her to serve it along with some rice that was popped and fried. Vanka sat in a corner searching for answers to the impending questions in his head. When Sonna had first arrived at the farm field looking for him, Vanka, who was resting under a tree at his farm field had no idea that his fate was at the crossroads. "Ley, Vanka! Some Tamil woman is at your house, claiming you are her husband!" Sonna's words had blocked his mind. While on the road home, he did not realise he had forgotten his bicycle; he really wanted to reach the inevitable destination as slowly as possible. Upon reaching his destination, the strange lady shrunk her face in dire need of his support, and Arobha went into the house with an irky face. When Venga arrived after his uncle, the skirmish on the street was stopped and everyone was moved into the house where Vanka now had everyone's faces turned against him. He was looking like a child who was caught robbing money from an elder's pocket, looking for an excuse to defend himself. When everyone started shooting him with questions, he stood blabbering like a school kid who was unprepared for the exam. Asobha intervened and asked everyone to be silent. "Give him a chance to explain himself," she said. "What is there to explain? His sins are standing so evidently in front of us." Venga retorted to Asobha's fine-grained tone with his hoarse voice. He had turned outraged after hearing the ignominious tale of his uncle from Aruna. "Son, whatever you think he has done, he is a human like all of us. Please let him speak on his own terms. Moreover, he is your elder and has been a father-figure your entire life." Asobha tried to calm her son. "I knew for a while that this man was onto something bad. From the time I had taken charge of selling the yield in the market, I have seen more profit than this man ever showed us. I am buying at least half an acre of land with the excess money gotten from every yield. Just imagine, what and all this man would have done with the money he syphoned off. How many more wives he is maintaining, only God knows!" Venga vented out. "Enough! Shut your mouth. Whom did you inform about the land you bought? Don't you know that in our family the land is always registered with women? How do we know tomorrow you will not do a similar thing and use the land you bought as a means of escape?" Vanka spoke befittingly, at which point Venga lost his cool. "After doing all these unspeakable things, now you are lecturing me?" Venga said in rage and moved towards Vanka raising his hands at which point Aruna stopped her husband. Even Asobha was hearing for the first time that Venga was making land purchases in his own name sans the knowledge of the women at home. Uncomfortable truths were coming out into the light. Asobha did not want to contribute to further revelations. Again, thinking of the unimagined turns of events that her family had taken, she laughed. When everyone froze to heed the laugh of the insane lady, she stopped her laugh and spoke, "You both should stop fighting now. Just listen to the cry of my sister and make up your mind to stop your nonsense for her sake at least." She tried to calm them both, pointing to the kitchen from where the continuous bickering voice of Arobha was heard.

"Venga, you very well know that from your grandmother's time, it has been a tradition in our house to own the land in the name of women. Your grandmother had her reasons and we have been following it as a tradition. Don't try to break it. In the next week, please transfer all the land in your name to Aruna. Otherwise, I am going to donate the land in my name to the village mutt." Venga looked annoyed, but Asobha's warning about donating the land to the mutt had stunned him. Asobha continued, "Now, addressing the elephant in the room, for whatever reason, Vanka has committed a mistake. But let us not forget that our problem involves a lone lady with a son. Whatever decisions we take will impact all of us along with them. So, I advise you to judge the situation with caution." She left the floor to others to speak. Arobha came out with rage and speed, and she started shouting at Vanka, "What have I done to you to punish me like this? You should have killed me instead. Haven't I fed you well? Haven't I satisfied you well? Haven't I taken care of your entire family well?" Vanka opened his mouth again. But he turned to Asobha and started speaking, "See, Asobha. I know she is your sister; hence you would hardly believe me after all these years. I alone know what I have been through after marrying your sister. At first, she was envious that my brother was better looking than me, and that you married a better-looking man than her. Later, from the day you bore Rama, she has been irksome about children. She has always been envious of your children and there is not a night that has passed without her pricking and emasculating words. She is not even close to you at heart." More revelations. If it was Asobha from a couple of years back, she would have reacted differently. After being visited by her mother-in-law and her elder son frequently in her dreams, and after having seen a lot to which she was blind before, any revelation seemed just like another day. '*She is not even close to you at heart*'. The last sentence from Vanka's words resounded in her mind for some reason and again, she laughed but at herself. Venga stopped addressing Asobha after she started laughing incessantly. While Arobha and Vanka's long course of bitter quarrel was on, Asobha went lost in her ponderings. She was realising how she was just as lost as she thought others were, in the play of life. She was realising how she was not even aware of her dear ones; forget the depths of life! When she came to her senses, Vanka was ready with his luggage packed, standing at the door, about to leave. Asobha feebly stood up and walked towards him, "Hey, Vanka, don't leave! Venga, stop him. Ask him not to leave." "Let him go. I will take care of my aunt. She doesn't need to be cared for by such a disgraced man," Venga replied to her, at which point she was close to him. She slapped him however feebly she could and said, "Enough! Enough of whatever you have already done and whatever you are doing now. Don't think I don't know your 'honourable' deeds. Just stop him, don't let this family fall further." She sounded affirmative. Venga looked to be cautioned by her words for a moment, but in a second, he ignored them for an insane lady's words, and then turning his face back into utter anger, he stormed out of the place into the backyard, saying, "He has heaped a lot of property and enough of a family from wherever that lady is from. He will be happy for sure. Let him be happy there. Why should our family take the fall and worry about his deeds?" She knew the source of his utterances. She knew the source of his attitude. She knew the source of his personality and choice of words. She saw herself. The source lied in the predilections of herself. The source of his behaviour lay in her upbringing. She could see everything from the past with crystal clarity. Even with the sea of knowledge and ocean of clarity, she could hardly quench her parched family. She started realising how helpless Vaisaki had felt in her days, in spite of having seen and known so much in life. In an attempt to vent herself out, Asobha laughed with tears. The laugh carried no happiness, and the tears carried no bliss. More such bursts of laughter were about to come which would push her into the zone of complete insanity in the eyes of onlookers, including her own family. People could see her outwardly but not what was running through her mind, just like she did with Rama and Vaisaki.

After Vanka's exit from the house, Arobha loomed into despair. She was not lively anymore, and every chore she performed had to be redone by someone else. Sometimes, she forgot what time it was, and sometimes, she forgot what she was doing and even why she was doing something. Sometimes, she would cry for no reason in the company of others, and sometimes, with no one around. Asobha tried to make time out of her tryst with the deceased, to console her little sister. But her sanity had lost credibility even in the eyes of the little sister, and whatever help she tried to offer, went unheeded. She didn't give up though. Every now and then, she walked out of her secluded room and entered the main house to offer visits to her little sister. She repeated it every day until it became a habit, at which point, Arobha decided to move back to Katilu. It was on the day when her nephew, Aguna and his wife, Rathi visited the house. Aruna had cooked up a festive meal for her brother and sister-in-law. After savouring the lunch, they sat down to munch on betel leaves and nuts. During munching, as a topic of conversation, the couple brought up their pregnancy. Easing into the conversation, they asked Arobha to accompany them to Katilu so that she could take care of Rathi, and at the same time, take some time off from the haunting memories of Bani village.

All along, it was Aruna's plan to send Arobha away for a while, to let her grasp a respite. A couple of weeks ago when Aruna was in Katilu, she had noticed that her sister-in-law had become pregnant, and at the same time, her mother had broken her leg falling from a precarious ladder. Aguna, the father-to-be, being worried for his wife, had asked his sister to look for a proper midwife from among the close relatives. When the debacle of Vanka happened, Asobha kept falling behind Arobha, asking her to find solace in God by visiting punya-kshetras. Arobha did not heed her advice and stayed frozen at home. That was when the thought of sending her back to Katilu struck Aruna's mind. Instantly, he sent a message to both Aguna and Rathi to visit Bani. And the events that followed landed Arobha in the cosy arms of her childhood home.

Every week, during her stay in Katilu, Arobha wrote letters to Aruna, inquiring about the welfare of her sister and nephew in the last and first lines of the writings. The remaining part, mostly, expressed the grief of her mind complaining about the agony of her soul. She resorted to letters instead of calling on the telephone. Writing letters felt more private, and also, writing gave her the luxury of time to find the apt words in her jumbled mind, which she could not do over the phone conversations. Sometimes, she wrote that she wished to be in Bani for the sake of her sister and sometimes, she wrote that she would never enter Bani for what Vanka reminded her of. Whenever Aruna read a letter, the grief in it would disturb her. Her attempt to keep Arobha away from Bani had not helped in keeping the aunt away from pain. However, she took respite in the fact that Arobha was busily engaged in helping Rathi most of the time, and her mental agony was restricted to the time of writing letters. With that thought in mind, she would re-read the letter, laugh at the petty grammar mistakes and the misdrawn alphabets, and she would continue engaging in her chores. She never encouraged Arobha to write more letters by responding to them. However, Arobha's letters kept raining.

After a while, a letter came. There were a few papers attached to the letter. Aruna started with the letter. With the usual 'aum' symbol and prologue of inquiring about everyone's welfare, she had directly jumped to the topic. "I am writing to you to inform you that hereby, all the property in my name, located in Bani, except for the seven guntas close to the house, will be yours. I have transferred the property to you and attached the related stamp papers. Take care of the further procedures. You don't have to come to Katilu, or I to Bani, for any trivial matters related to the land. I want at least you to be happy." The letter continued. But Aruna had stopped minding the rest of the letter, though she was reading just for the sake of it. In bewilderment, she dialled to her home in Katilu immediately. Even after talking to Arobha on the phone, she was not convinced. For that matter, she was more bewildered after talking to Arobha. Especially, when Aruna asked her if Vaidhe should be named for half of all the possessions of the family. '*That woman who did not even turn out for her own husband's cremation? She is not our family. And, I always had a feeling that she was never part of our family. She showed her true colours anyway. Forget her. Take care of your husband and your son.*' Aruna recalled Arobha's words on the phone in exact order, word by word. Every time she recalled, she could see the reason in Arobha's frustration, but that didn't stop her from wondering what might be going on in Vaidhe's head. It was the question she had been asking since the day of Rama's cremation. But she had no clue to even fathom. She had not even heard gossip about her since the day of the cremation. Apparently, Vaidhe's relatives in Bani had gone dead silent since Rama's death.

It was hard for Sukha to tolerate and evade cross-questioning by the village folk on his family's despair. But it was him, if anyone could do it. It was out of his repentance that he tolerated the utter and obvious nonsense. The guilt of being the primary person responsible for setting Vaidhe and Rama's match would never evade him. There wasn't a single day that had passed without regretting his decision to help Vaidhe, in her endeavour to marry Rama. But, what else could he have done at that moment? The glimmer of hope in the eyes of the lost niece made him do what he did.

16
Twilight at the Dusk

On a tender morning of the winter, the dream of Vaidhe seemed to have laid down the carpet, inviting all the guests to witness the ceremony. As Rama walked along the path to the *mandapam*, he couldn't miss noticing the dew drops on the leaves of the guava tree. Even on such an important day of his life, he was taken back to his childhood. It reminded him of that particular day, in his initial days of learning tree climbing, where he was drawn by dew droplets on the leaves of a guava tree. The mind had a desire to climb the tree and pluck a fruit off the tree, with the drops of dew still embellishing the fruit. That day had taught him the perils of dew drops while climbing the tree. He had taken an almost deadly fall due to the slippery branches of the guava tree, caused by the dew drops while attempting to reach for the fruit. The metaphor seemed to have been lost on him. Coming out of childhood memory, he entered the *mandapam* and sat for the conduct of rituals. The much gossiped about marriage of Rama with Vaidhe had drawn a large crowd, mostly from the confines of the village. Some of them were there in awe, some for the formality of attending the wedding, and some to validate if what they heard was indeed true. Some spoke about how an insane guy like Rama could also get a bride to marry, some spoke about how ridiculous it was for Shunka's family to marry a widow into the family, and some even genuinely blessed Rama and Vaidhe on the occasion. Regardless, all the murmurs and sounds of thoughts, of the people gathered, were dissolved into nothingness by the sounds of *peepi* and percussion.

Asobha had planned to conduct both the sons' marriage at the same time and venue, just as Arobha and she were married off to Vaisaki's sons. She dropped the plan upon being advised by a few against it as a bad omen. 'It is bad luck to conduct two marriages under the same *mandapam*, unless it involves twins. Else, at least one marriage will be in ruins,' one person said. 'It is not good for the genetic propagation of family trees if two marriages are conducted on the same *muhurtha*. That is what made Arobha and Vanka childless,' another said. Few others had their own reasoning, ranging from having to bear crippled children to having to bear children who would cripple the family. One person was categorically blunt in invoking the death of Raju in the face of Asobha, attributing it as a consequence of twin marriage. Listening to all the grave examples, Asobha had to surrender her intention of conducting a twin marriage. She convinced her brother Atura and his wife, Rani, to have the marriage of Venga and Aruna soon, but at a later time.

The match between Venga and Aruna was in the making for a long time. The only thing that was detrimental to Asobha and Atura's plan of alliance was Rama's marriage, which was about to be done with. They had to just wait a couple of months more to further reinforce their genetic bond through the matrimony of their children. After the *muhurtha*, while sitting with a group of ladies for a casual talk, the topic of Venga's marriage was invoked. Asobha started to see Venga's marriage as if it was happening in front of her eyes, under the same *mandapam*. Her eyes welled up in the next few seconds at the imagined reality. The ladies, who had surrounded Asobha, started to attribute her tears to the perceived relief on the occasion of completing her elder son's marriage – which, in their sense, could make any mother well up, given the elder son was Rama. Asobha did not repudiate the attribution.

Sukha, having taken charge of his niece's remarriage, put his body and soul into executing the ceremony. He had not had proper rest in the past few days. Yet, he stayed as zealous as he could be, throughout. His sister, Suneena and her family had lent their share of hands to the chores. After the marriage, when Rama and Vaidhe had to leave for Maithalli for the groom's reception at the bride's house, Sukha got the respite he deserved. He ate a large meal, drank a big bowl of buttermilk – ignoring the winter – and slept like an ox which had just finished ploughing acres of land. He was never so satisfied in his life. Suneena, after a long time, circumambulated Bani to invite all her relatives to her house, before she took off to Maithalli with the newlywed couple. The bride and the groom had already taken off in Byrappa's Tata Sumo, which he personally had cleaned and arranged for his dear Rama to commute during and around the marriage ceremonies. In the afternoon, the herd from Maithalli marched back home. The herd was trying to decide whether to take the public bus or to wait for the pre-arranged tempo. '*Hey, that bus travels all the way around and into the town of Klar. As if that is not enough, it rests there for a while before leaving for Maithalli. By that time, I can easily finish two rounds of to and fro trips to my home by walk.*' An old man said before choosing the mode of journey, and those who heeded his words with a laugh had accompanied him in the wait for the tempo; a very few, who had been impatient or repellent to the turmoil of the tempo travel, had taken the bus anyway.

By the time the bus reached Maithalli, the bride and groom were sitting on the bench, and those who had chosen tempo were already at the venue with their ritual plates. And as usual, the function went into the late night, and the first night of consummation – though they did not consummate – went into the early morning. Rama made sure he slept on the floor, away from the bed and distant from Vaidhe. On that first night, she did not question why. She remained silent along with him. On the next day, after arriving for the bride's reception at Bani, the family could not help but notice the obvious silence and aloofness of Rama with his wife. Even when Vaidhe wanted to ask something, she would address him with indirect colloquials – 'See here...', 'What means...'. By the tone of her ask, he was supposed to know that it was him she was addressing. While most of the gathered family attributed their way of talking to the shyness of a newly married couple, his family from the house knew it was more than that. However, they were least interested in the connotations of those colloquials. In any marriage, the couple was supposed to explore and establish their own style of communication. With time, it was bound to happen. On the night of the bride's reception, Vaidhe almost broke into a fight with one of the village ladies who tried to be funny by passing an obscene comment on Rama. It was then that Rama realised that Vaidhe was not at all coerced into the marriage like he was. It was then that he felt her concern – if not love – for him. With that little spark in mind, he went into the bedroom on his second night. He slept on the floor to the left of the bed, turning left on his side. As on the previous night, Vaidhe moved to the edge of the bed and slept on her left side gazing at Rama. After a while, Rama rolled to his right to sleep up-straight. The moonlight from the window had lit up his face bright and blue. Vaidhe flowered with a tingling. '*At least I can talk to your face today,*' she murmured and smiled within. Millions of words were said to his face which travelled into the night only to be acknowledged by the crickets.

The third night saw Vaidhe coming up with a plan to make Rama talk. She had preoccupied his sleeping spot on the floor. She wished he would at least notice her effort to earn his attention. When Rama saw her on the floor, instead of on the bed, he came close to her and patted slightly on her shoulder. '*Why are you sleeping on the floor? It is not the right place for you. Please, use the bed.*' '*No problem. If you can sleep here, I too can.*' She had mustered all the courage and wrapped her words in the most soothing moan. He could not resist turning soft on her. After a few more words, they wound up sleeping together on the bed. Rama, like someone who had just realised something, said, "I thought you would be averse to this marriage, and I didn't peg you for being interested in me. Were you or not coerced into this marriage?" "No. There was nothing like coercion et al. In fact, I was the one who, in a way, planned our marriage." Her words struck him in the strangest way, soothing his heart. It was not just the knowledge that someone intentionally wanted to be with him, but also that someone wanted to be with him for life, and that too as his spouse, with whom he would be wrapped and confined in a room for almost half of the life to come. He moved a little closer to her and she to him. "*I didn't know you liked me,*" Rama said to her as she snared him with her stare. She then snuggled him into bliss.

They curled up into each other in many ways they themselves never knew of. In an attempt to get to know each other, they had become one. The envious full moon from the clear sky was trying to peek through the window to bear witness to the convergence and was, in futility, hooking rays of moonlight to steal the romance away from the room. A love was forged into life on that night.

✦

It was no season for haggling. Nature had profusely yielded. Bees were confused to pick the flowers among the lot. Birds fought no more for their place in the lush trees. Monkeys could make the journey through the trees from one end of the village to the other without being seen. The cattle were munching varieties of grass. Farmers were reaping their crops well. Villagers had plenty to offer each other through their deities. Even the street dogs found lots of unfinished tasty food in every dump of the village. Everybody had something to take without bothering others of their kind. In such a bountiful state of nature, Rama was bestowed with Vaidhe. Within no time, they had become another pair of birds who just lived dancing to the tune of inadvertent love. And, within no time came the wedding of Venga and Aruna too.

Venga had just sold the entire yield from the farming – potatoes from one and a half acres of the upper layer of fields, tomatoes from an acre of the lower layer of fields, rice grain from the *kaane* – and he had submitted the earnings, along with the accounting, to his mother and uncle. There was a steep increase in the earnings compared to what Vanka had earned the last time he was in charge, from almost the same commensurate amount of land and crops. Vanka didn't waste any time in attributing the gains to the auspicious time of Venga's charge-taking. Asobha was mindful in discreetly dividing the credit to both Venga and Vaidhe – the auspicious time of Venga's charge-taking and the auspicious time of Vaidhe's entry into the family. However, Rama was kept unattended in a corner of her heart just as he was kept in the corner of the house erstwhile. Nonetheless, she was happy that the house received money in the need of the hour, and a boost in the earnings had boosted her into extravagantly conducting Venga's marriage with her niece. The hands of the Kubja Vengadi family had joined the Shunka family in squandering the money more precariously to tune the ceremony into their perceived prestige. Asobha went all her lengths and breadths to keep up the conduct of the occasion to the pride of the Kubja Vengadi family via Shunka's family. She welcomed Aruna like a mother – a mother who is bereft of lactation, inviting a cow into the house. Asobha's dream of a treasured woman arriving from the Kubja Vengadi family, just like she arrived a generation ago, to set right the pride of Shunka's family to its glory through her deeds, was coming to fruition. To the one who was intensely invested in dreams and whims, the best of them were taking shape.

✦

With two daughters-in-law at home, Asobha was put in the same place as Vaisaki from a generation ago. But, unlike Asobha and Arobha, her daughters-in-law were not siblings and, Aruna was from her own bloodline whereas Vaidhe was not. Though Asobha tried to balance her extroverted love for both Vaidhe and Aruna, her inherent love always tilted in favour of the latter. Whenever the daughters-in-law went away to their native homes to celebrate the festivals with their bloodline in the first year, as per the customs, Asobha only cared to share pleasantries on the phone with Aruna, not Vaidhe. She would insist Aruna return home as she missed her absence in the house, while she insisted Vaidhe return home as and when there was a need to conduct the household work. If she bought a set of bangles for her daughters-in-law, she would add an extra *jhumka* for Aruna, and when bought a set of *jhumka*, she would add an extra nose pin for her. And with Arobha in the house, it did not take long to reveal the bias of Asobha. However, Vaidhe never minded such unworthy details. From the depth of an abyss, she had already claimed the biggest mountain of her life and had landed in the arms of Rama. Everything else seemed petty. She was so busy exploring life with Rama that she had no time for her parents either. Whenever she was asked by Asobha to visit Maithalli for the festivals in the first year, Vaidhe would stay back with made-up excuses of farm work or house chores, though Rama was her real excuse. However, Rama would insist she visit her parents by explaining how the tradition of first-year festival visits came into being and how it would quell the plight of – not only the new bride but also – her parents who would be looming in her absence. Heeding his words, she visited Maithalli a few times, but without heart. Sometimes, she would ask Rama to stay with her when he accompanied her to Maithalli to drop off, but he would always insist on returning back to Bani to attend to the farm work. Their romance was not lost at any moment. Even in the absence of each other's company, they kept it alive in the longing.

After all the other festivals of the year, came the time of Dussehra. Both Rama and Vaidhe just finished offering prayers to all their ancestors of the Shunka family on the day of *Mahalaya Amavasya* and left for Maithalli. This time, at the receiving end, Vaidhe's mother was hell-bent on making her daughter stay for all ten days of the festival. In preparation, she had asked her to reach Maithalli before the first day of *Navaratri* so that they could start the festival together with the first day's *vrata*. Vaidhe had agreed to stay upon reaching her parents' home, she held back Rama too for a couple of days. Rama had to stay back at her stubborn insistence. He called home and asked Vanka to look after his crop in his absence.

The house of his in-laws was a little cold on that day, compared to the warmth on the night of the groom's reception. There was not much conversation with the in-laws. Varna also seemed to be busy with usual affairs as he had made himself scarce at home. Revi, Varna's wife, was helping her mother-in-law along with Vaidhe in preparing the house for the coming festivities. In the face of utter silence elsewhere, Rama constricted himself to the bedroom. Vaidhe would join him after finishing all her chores.

One morning, stepping out of the house, Rama plucked a twig from the neem tree in front of the house. Brushing his teeth with it, he took a walk towards the in-laws' farm fields. While taking the walk, he reminisced about his vagabond days and recalled several of his visits to the village of Maithalli. Not even once had he thought that someday his journey would end up there. Laughing at the play of life as he usually did, he walked back to the house. On his way back, he noticed how the village had still kept alive the haystack huts, bathing cubes made by braiding coconut branches into one another, outdoor grinding stones, threshing rock rollers, et al. However, his village, Bani, had upgraded over time and had foregone all those beautiful antic innovations. Though his upgraded village stood in contrast to Maithalli, the role of stray dogs in the play of village life hadn't changed anywhere. When he was about a furlong from his in-law's house, he saw a dog sniffing and rustling the leaves of the coconut bathing cube. It was pushing its muzzle into the bathing cube as if it had smelled a bone from inside. A lady, who apparently was bathing inside, called, "Who is that?" Her harsh voice made the dog take a toll on its feet, and it ran around the bathing cube towards the road, flapping its limbs in the swamp created by the bathing cube outlet. The lady in the bathing cube stood up to check out. She missed the dog and saw Rama – the Rama who was smiling, not at her but at the jest of the event he had just witnessed – where a lady had mistaken a dog for a person. He walked away.

Entering the backyard of his in-laws' house, throwing away the neem stick, he went into the bathroom and finished the cold-water bath. He visited the temple of the village and sat there for a while. The interested folk of the village had a word or two to acquaint with the new groom of the village on their way to work. He smilingly replied or confirmed his identity. The hour passed and he returned home where his in-laws awaited him. "Rama, it is time for you to leave. You must be having a lot of work at home." Jana insisted. Rama was slightly confused. He was not sure if that was an order or request. Moreover, Vaidhe was absent. Something did not add up. When he asked for Vaishe, Jana replied that she was at the farm field with Suneena. Against his comfort, he had to leave Maithalli at the insistence of his father-in-law. He could not overstay the in-law's invitation, especially after being asked to vacate with such blunt words.

When Vaidhe and her mother returned home from the farm field with a basin full of flowers and tulsi leaves, she inquired for Rama to serve him breakfast. Jana informed her that he left the house excusing himself with some important work. She was a little upset. '*Even after insisting so much, he did not stay. He could have at least bid goodbye before leaving.*' She said to herself. Jana took his wife into the bedroom and closed the door from behind. Sitting next to her, he whispered into her. "Devika was here earlier." "Hmm, what about her?" she asked back. Taking a deep breath, he continued to gut out whatever he wanted to gut out, "She complained that Rama was peeking while she was taking a bath." Suneena was outraged, instantly. She immediately stood up and moved to the door. Jana knew what she was up to. He intervened and brought her back. "This is a sensitive issue. Don't act hastily and blow it out of proportion." Jana warned. "Knowing Devika, she would have already informed Vengala and Koyal from her neighbourhood. Do you really think I would blow it out of proportion?" She said, staring at him angrily – at which point Jana released her hand. She walked straight out of the house without heeding Revi's offering of *prasadam*. She strode straight to Devika's home.

ꕥ✦ꕥ

"Tell me the truth!" Suneena demanded from Devika, standing in front of the portrait of gods and placing her hand on the lit lamp. Devika replied, "If I say anything that is not true, let my tongue fall down." She narrated the incident she witnessed when she was taking a bath in the morning, inside the bathing cube – walled by wooden sticks and coconut branches neatly intertwined and braided on all four sides, maintaining the continuity and obscuring the visibility. "In the morning, after cleaning the house and readying everything for *vrata*, I went to pour a couple of bowls of water on the body. During the shower, I heard the rustling of the leaves on the side of the wall to the road. Somebody was trying to pierce a hole in the leaves to peek. I shouted, 'Who is that?'. Hearing my sound that pervert tried to escape. I heard the footsteps and stood up to find out who it was. I saw your son-in-law standing on the road, a few feet away, looking at me and smiling. I could not stop myself from boiling from the bottom to the top at that wicked smile. Had I not been bathing and had he not been your in-law, I would have taught him a lesson then and there. Anyway, after the bath, I had time to think it through. Your son-in-law is from a far-off village. He will be here today and leave tomorrow. But we have to face each other and mingle with each other daily. So, I felt like telling it to brother Jana instead of creating a ruckus out of it." Suneena held both the hands of Devika in a gesture of solemn gratitude and left her house.

"Can you please call his mother and talk to her about it? Someone must put a check on this man. Otherwise, he will devour our honour in no time!" Suneena said to Jana. They did not have a telephone at home. They were supposed to use a neighbour's phone if they were to call anyone. "This is a sensitive matter. It is not prudent to use a neighbour's phone to delegate such a matter. Let me visit them once tomorrow," said Jana, turned to his other side and closed his eyes. However, the turbulence in his mind evaded the sleep and kept him awake through the night.

17
In The Name of Honour

Venga was sitting on the main bench at the village gate, chit-chatting with his gregarious gossip-gang. Kushika, a lady from the down-street of the village, passed in front of the gang. She turned slightly towards the gang, threw a subtle smile and walked away. "Who was she smiling at?" asked Venga. "She would smile at any man," replied Madhu, one among the gang. The gang burst into laughter. "I heard a rumour that someone is boinking her," Venga threw the gossip wide open. "Yes, down-street Ragappa caught her romancing with someone in the bushes near his farm field. Looks like the guy ran away before he could catch his face. Alas! This girl got stuck in the bushes!" Koli narrated. "Does her father know about her saga?" Venga asked again. "Who knows? Perhaps he will hear it when he starts looking for a groom." The gang burst into laughter again. When the laughter receded, Venga said "Whatever you say, whores like this ruin our village's name. If I am to catch her with that man again, I will chase that bastard and beat him to death first." "You watch out for your family's honour first. You can look after the village later," Madhu kindled with him. The conversation continued with heat and laughter. Within a while, the bus stopped at the village gate and from it, Jana descended. "Hm, the big man from the Maithalli is here. I will leave now." Venga bid adieu to the chit-chatting and went to attend to Jana. He escorted him home. On the way, Jana took an excuse from Venga to visit his brother-in-law, Sukha's house. Venga dropped him off at Sukha's house and went to his home. Jana spent hardly an hour at Sukha's. After handing over clothes that he had brought as festival gifts to Sukha and his spouse, he took off with an excuse to visit Asobha's house.

At Asobha's house, Jana was hesitant to open the obvious and uncomfortable conversation. To have a minimum audience, he requested to speak with Asobha alone. Asobha warded off his concern about Venga's presence, praising him as her most reliable person on the earth. He spit out Devika's story along with the concerns of Suneena. Asobha turned outraged. At first, she dared Jana not to make false accusations about her family's honour. But later she succumbed to Jana's reasoning behind his doubts. In his reasoning, he was not reticent in bringing up the incident of Rama and his daughter from their childhood as they had witnessed. It was sufficient for Asobha to tilt on the side of error, into believing that Rama could have committed such a disgusting act of trying to peek into a bathing cube. "It's up to you, however you want to proceed with this. I have a request though. For the next few months, don't send my daughter to my home in his company. If you wish to send her, she can come alone... And, I have told everyone in the village that I have come to Bani to offer new clothes to Sukha and his wife on behalf of my wife. You can maintain the same story if you want." Jana, after shooting the long list of well-prepared words with utmost clarity and tone, left Asobha's home and then Bani. Even after his exit, his words, which had turned into a noose, were suffocating Asobha. Venga stood against the wall in the same position, like a statue, as he did while Jana was in. "What should we do, mother?" asked Venga. "I don't know. I don't know if we can do anything. But I am sure we can't keep quiet too. Go, find him and bring him at once!" she commanded. Venga left the house like a messenger who was out for deliverance.

✦

In the hinterland of the forest, which had lined the border of the village, was the major portion of farm fields that belonged to Shunka's family. After Shunka, Vaisaki had expanded them with her earnings. After a generation, Venga tried to expand it further. By the time Venga took over, the fields on both the upper tranche and lower tranche surrounded by the forest on two sides and roads on the other two, belonged to Shunka's family. At the feet of the forest, in the middle of the two tranches, was a water well with an attached powerhouse. The round well, which was dug by Shunka along with his mining friends was well walled and staircased till the bottom, using the rocks extracted from the hills of Avali. Hence, the rock stood afresh even after several decades. Shunka had also built a powerhouse on one side of the well. It had a rectangular pit in a corner which opened into the well at its bottom at about one-sixth of the depth of the well. In the olden days, when Mother Earth was gracious, the well used to swell to its fullest and the pit inside the powerhouse also filled up along with the well. A motor, installed inside the powerhouse that contained and secured other farming tools, would be placed near the pit to pump the water from the well. But with time, the water level had sunk. At the third generation, even with water pumped out from nearby borewells being released into it, the water never reached half mark. With the motor descended deep into the well to match the existing levels of water, the pit in the powerhouse was left abandoned. While the powerhouse had a door, the opening of the pit into the well, which was left unclosed, provided another way into the powerhouse via the stairs of the well. This was the path that the bees, birds and lovers in the village chose to build their nest in the forsaken pit.

Madhu and Kushika were in the pit, involved in their affair as usual. But this time, as soon as they met, Madhu warned Kushika about the conversation he had had earlier that day with his gossip-gang. They mutually decided to find another spot to meet then-after. After his cautionary chat, he switched to the usual charade of lingering on his lust, biting her every part, top to bottom, with his lips and attributing the taste to distinct fruits. When he was about to slide below her neck, she interrupted. "What happened?" he asked. "I hear someone coming," she replied. Madhu turned his attention to the sound that Kushika seemed to have heard. The rustling of the dry leaves revealed that someone was walking towards the powerhouse.

It was Rama. He was at the fields, investigating the soil for his next crop to be sown. While at it, he saw several dry branches in the coconut trees which he decided to bring down for firewood. He was going to the powerhouse to fetch the tools he needed. The love birds went dead silent when Rama entered the powerhouse. He picked up his tools and exited. As soon as they heard Rama's footsteps fading away, Madhu asked Kushika to sneak out of the pit via the stairs of the well. Kushika slowly snuck out of the pit, climbed the stairs of the well and surreptitiously tiptoed on the other side of the powerhouse keeping an eye on Rama in order not to fall into his sight. After tiptoeing and circling halfway around the well, she collided with Venga who was there in search of Rama.

Kushika, confused and terrified like a thief caught in the action, ran away without turning back. Venga walked around the well to check if he could catch the secret man around. Madhu, who was about to sneak out of the pit from the bottom opening, saw Venga at the top of the well. Recollecting Venga's words from that morning – *"If I am to catch her with that man again, I will chase that bastard and beat him to death first"* - he snuck back into the pit like a tortoise sneaking its head into the shell. When Venga went around the well, he saw Rama walking away from the powerhouse on the other side. At that moment, when he was already in fury from what Jana had narrated at this house, what he saw was sufficient to corroborate his conjecture that it was Rama who was fooling around with Kushika. Thunderstruck by his own conjecture, he involuntarily walked back, crossed the farm fields, walked down the dusty road and sat down on a stone bench, pondering over. The silence of the wind took him back to his school days. When his classmates had come to know of the delinquent Rama's act of kissing, as his brother, he bore the brunt of his classmates for Rama's action. During any argument regarding any matter, his classmates drew flare at him quoting his brother's deed. *'You are the brother of a pervert, what else can be expected of you'* - was the common dialogue that everyone used as a final weapon against him, during any fight or argument, which he never knew how to armour against. He was so fed up with the taunting that in a couple of years, succumbing to his pressure, Vanka had to change his school to a nearby town with the pretext of better schooling. He reminisced about the past which he was never responsible for but was forced to be a part of. In addition to the past, he recalled the words of Jana earlier in his house. As if something came on him, he stood and strode with the wind. He went back to the powerhouse. He could not find Rama. He saw the shepherd, Ranga, who was grazing his sheep in the open field in the upper tranche. He looked to be waving at someone at a distance who looked like Rama and was walking away with what seemed like a sack in his hand. He took the inner route via Byrappa's fields and surreptitiously followed Rama from a distance.

Along his surreptitious walk, many thoughts crawled through the creepy brain of the younger brother. Some of the thoughts, however disconcerting, were beckoning calm and reasoning. But most of them were rumbling haste and hate. He approached the swampy rice fields across which was the embankment of the pond. In the middle of it, under the jamun tree, he could see a man whose shape resembled that of Rama sitting. He tiptoed on the narrow passages through the rice fields. While tiptoeing, he made room in his mind for a plan of action. He had a clear idea of what he wanted to do and how to do it. As he approached the person, he confirmed that the person sitting was whom he intended. He picked up a thick log which had a protuberance near the farther end. Slowly climbing onto the embankment, he reached behind Rama without being noticed. Holding the log with sheer grip, he hit the back of his skull. The protuberance pierced into the skull, and the sound of cracking delegated the inevitability of death to the air around.

Before he could pluck the dry branches from the coconut trees, Rama saw the flock of sheep appearing at a furlong, along with its shepherd. "O Ranga, bring them here," Rama called, and Ranga obliged. "Let your flock feed here. It would help reduce the weed in my field," said Rama.

"Rama, did you have lunch?"

"No."

"Take my sack and have it."

"What about you?"

"I attended a function at a friend's house in Arali. When I went grazing my sheep on that side, I saw a fresh canopy and flower decoration at a house. Just out of curiosity, I went nearby to inquire. To my surprise, my friend came out. It was his in-laws' house. His son's naming ceremony, it was. Whatever the chef made was very good. I had a blissful meal. With my stomach full, how could I eat another sack of food? See my bloated stomach." Ranga unveiled a torrent of words along with his bulging stomach.

"Ha ha. Bless you. Give the sack. What's in it?" Rama inquired.

"I smell wild-spice chutney in the morning. My wife would have turned all her anger into spice and prepared wild-spice chutney. As if that wasn't enough, she would have put a couple of green chillies. The ragi-lump seems to be small. Rub less chutney with each bite. She would have kept a couple of shallots. Pluck a few more from Byrappa's crop. Else, you won't be able to bear the spice." Ranga spit out the tenets to consume his wife's food. Rama threw his usual smile and walked away. "Where are you going?" Ranga asked. Rama just waved his hand to the north and walked away.

On the embankment of the pond stood a jamun tree facing the light while the sun wavered between the horizons. The late afternoon was still fiery and had cast the shadow of the tree onto the bank. That was where Rama sat to savour the fiery lunch. He was already late. His stomach was beating with the rhythm of hunger. He opened the sack, recollecting Ranga's warnings. Rama had tasted a lot of local cuisines from several many villages. In one place, sambar was cooked sweet using jaggery. In another place, chilli powder with a spoon of ghee was served as sambar. Having seen the extremes of spice, he had brushed Ranga's warning away with a smile. Forget extra, he needed no shallots to quell any spice. The bite of ragi-lump mixed with the chutney was sliding from the watering mouth straight into the stomach, leaving its signature of spice on the tongue. Every bite was invited by a burst of saliva and with every bite, the tongue was seeking more. Covered by the shade of jamun and being blown by the cold wind running along the surface of the pond water, the spicy bites tasted like drops of elixir even in the fiery afternoon. The clouds started to loom, bearing brunt witness to the dying evening. Like a tornado that could shatter even the most serene landscape, something struck the back of his head and he collapsed instantly.

From childhood, Venga was intuitive in his plan of action. Once, when he had stolen money from his uncle's pocket and had used it to pay for a school trip that he desired, he had gotten caught by the puny gossip that reached back home from the school. However, he had managed to convince him that he had found that money on the road outside the house, not in the pocket of his uncle, and that he paid that money towards the rest of his school fees, not for the school trip. Of course, he had all the time in the world to convert the school trip fees to school fees on the next day. Another time, he had shrewdly chosen the apt situation to push his classmate into some thorny bushes. He chose the time when there was a bull, crossing by that classmate and he had pushed him on the pretext of saving him from a bull attack, while his actual intention was seeking revenge for vile name-calling. In privy, many more such acts had borne witness to his knack for whim with impunity in the past.

Standing unshaken on the embankment, Venga placed the log on the ground where blood was spilled, and then, he slid Rama in order to place his head close to the log. Sitting on forefeet, bending down with the support of his palms and placing his head above Rama's, Venga looked straight up to the tree to identify the most direct branch on the tree at an apt height. After investigating, he picked up the food sack with whatever was left in it, quickly climbed the tree and broke the identified branch at its joint. Dropped the sack of food from the top, on the ground close to where Rama was lying. Leaving the broken branch to hang, he climbed down the tree, removed Rama's necklace and bracelet for his backup plan of 'robbery gone havoc', looked around for any hints of witnesses, and then vacated the place leaving no clue. He made sure he kept himself available in the vicinity to reach the spot when he heard the hue and cry. When Ranga identified Rama's body later that evening, it was easy for Venga to reach the spot. He reached the spot, looked up at the tree and passed his first judgement, "One more death in my family to tree climbing." Eventually, that narrative was propagated by the rest as the cause of death. The narrative took its own course through the gossip of the village and served towards vindicating him. Who could blame gossip for its lack of sense? Venga did not need his backup plan of 'robbery gone havoc' anymore. He wanted to bury the ornaments somewhere before they were melted for reuse. He kept them close to him till the *tharpana*. On the night of tharpana, he found the right place in the backyard of his house. Initially, he thought of putting them into a small sack and sticking it in the corner roof of the shed. Later, bolstering his plan, he removed the waste boxes from one of the corners on the ground, dug up the ground, buried the necklace and the bracelet, and covered the corner with mud and boxes.

18
The Legacy

On the day of *tharpana*, the third day from the day of Rama's demise, the truth attempted to beckon through a whisper. When the congregation dispersed after the libation of milk, from the grave where the ashes were buried, Asobha had relapsed into the darkness of her room. At some point in the night, in search of a breeze, she approached the bars of the window. Camouflaged by the darkness around and within her, in that gloomy snuggery, she noticed the light in the backyard shed turned on. Venga went into the shed with a small sack in his hand. She heard a few sounds, including that of digging, for a minute. After a while, she saw Venga coming out of the shed empty-handed and switching off the lights. The intrigued mind did not wait for long. It tried to dig the doubts from the corner of the shed, and it found out. It was Rama's ornaments! '*Why did he have to hide them? After all, they belonged to his brother,*' she thought. Then, her mind recalled not seeing any ornaments on his body when Venga, along with villagers, had brought the body to the house. The mystery around the ornaments started to unfold several conjectures in her mind. And, that one conjecture, she really wanted not to be true. She decided to fact-check. Keeping the ornaments under the bed at the headrest, she waited for the right time.

A clue came running in search of her. Ranga, the shepherd, was walking his path with his sheep in front of Asobha's house when he made up his mind to visit the bereaved mother and offer her a few consoling words along with a munch of betel nuts and leaves. After all, it was just the second day after her son had died. "*Rama would have done the same for my mother,"* he thought. He asked his day partner, Niga, to look after his sheep as he entered Asobha's house for a chat over betel leaves. Arobha pointed him to the desolate room inside the house. When he entered the room, Asobha sat on her bed looking outside the window. In the conversation that followed, that was where Ranga brought up the topic of Rama. "I spoke to him an hour before I found him dead. I am not just saying because you are his mother, but how shining he was when I saw him the last time. Just to pull his leg, I asked him what his in-laws gave as a wedding gift. He pulled out his thick neck chain out of his shirt and showed off. To that, I told him, '*No gold shines like your golden smile.*' He left alive from there; in a few hours, he was no longer alive. He still reminds me of himself with that smile." After the death of Rama, Asobha had become accustomed to hearing good things from the villagers about her son. Some things sounded trivial, but some things surprised her. The mother was getting to know her son after his death. But she attributed all the good talk to the usuality of kindness towards the dead. After all, no one speaks ill of the dead. But one thing that Ranga mentioned hit her mind. "*He pulled out his neck chain...*" Once Ranga was finished praising Rama, she pushed her words slowly into the chatter, "When did you arrive at his dead body? Was there anyone at the place before you?"

"Niga was grazing his herd on the other side of the pond. I was grazing them in your upper tranche. We were to meet on our way back. I saw Rama first while walking on the embankment. After that came Venga."

"Did you happen to see anyone removing the neck chain from Rama's neck?"

"No. I did not see anyone. I helped move the body into the village. I stayed with the body until it was cremated. I don't recall removing the chain anywhere. Why do you ask? Is it lost?"

"Ha... I don't know. I do think so," she responded in a way to keep Ranga aloof in the matters of Rama's ornaments.

"Who cleaned the body before cremation?"

"I was there along with other women. I was just curious if you saw anyone remove his ornaments before he was brought here."

"No, mother! I did not take them for sure. I did not see anyone taking them too."

"Someone in the family would have taken and kept them. It is okay. Don't worry about them. When the person itself is gone, what to do with the ornaments?" She tried to further brush away the topic of ornaments.

All Asobha needed to know was if he saw Venga taking them off after he went to Rama's body. She couldn't ask it directly. But Ranga had already confirmed what she wanted to know. Now she knew when the ornaments reached the hands of Venga. The horror slowly crept into her mind. From then on, she started losing herself.

She had several plans to confront Venga to extract the truth of Rama's death. But, within a short time, Aruna announced her pregnancy. Venga was not just a son or a husband anymore. He was going to be a father to a progeny. Even in the destitute of grieving a son, the bereaved mother was put to the test of weighing a murderous son against a prospective father. Asobha locked the truth within herself, stopping her line of inquiry. She suffered silently with the knowledge of horrors she had groomed all her life. From there on, it did not take long for Vaisaki and Rama to creep into her dreams. The moral tales of Vaisaki were only matched – in their pinching – by the silence of Rama. She understood his beckoning silence but did not give up her attempts to make him talk. She held her breath, awaiting the sound of Rama. Even in the middle of the turmoil, her mind could conspire a plan to leave behind something in the memory of Rama. She arranged for a trustworthy lawyer with the help of Byrappa and wrote a will in secret. She left all her earthly possessions to Vaidhe, Rama's wife. She knew that Venga could not fight it in the court, as the property owned in her name was bought by her, or donated to her by Vaisaki, none was recorded as inherited. "With regard to all my earthly possessions, Vaidhe – the wife of my elder son, Rama – will be the sole owner, upon my death. It is not to say that I am leaving Aruna with nothing. I know Aruna can inherit the possessions of Arobha and the property bought hereafter." The lawyer who had no qualms with Asobha's family did well to keep the will confidential.

On a fine night, Rama appeared alone in her dream. He sat near the hundred-year-old peepal tree on the midway to Shunka's farm fields. Asobha approached him from behind. As he heard her footsteps, he turned back and smiled at her, still no words. He pointed her to the tree. She looked with curiosity. The pointing finger pushed her attention to a tender leaf. As she was looking at that one leaf, a dry twig fell from above, cutting the leaf down. As the leaf kept falling, a small whirlwind came swirling and sucked the leaf into it. As the whirlwind moved away, it grew stronger and stronger. After rounding up the place around, the whirlwind sped towards Asobha and died. The leaf finally fell at Asobha's feet. She lifted it with her hand. The fallen leaf, which was tender when broken from the twig, had dried with several ruptures in it. She turned to Rama in pain, hoping he would speak to her a word or two. He just smiled intensely and disappeared into thin air. Opening her eyes from the dream, Asobha cried her heart out. Hearing the soul-waking cry, both Venga and Aruna rushed into her room in the backyard. "What happened now?" asked Venga. She looked at him with loathing regret. She turned to Aruna and said, "Don't ever let your son grow by himself, and more importantly, keep him away from this man as much as possible." Aruna looked confused. Asobha put her hand under the bed and pulled a sack from underneath, handed it over to Venga and said, "I know what you did." Venga was bewildered and sat frozen. "It's alright. I haven't told anyone. And I will not. I don't want your child to be fatherless like you and Rama were. There is a price our family has been paying for generations, bereavement at the hand of fate. If you don't want a similar fate to envelop your child, you stay away from its life and Vaidhe's. And you..." She turned to Aruna and said, "Make sure you limit this man's influence in your child's life. And you too, give only love, nothing more and nothing less. That is all. Go to sleep." Venga and Aruna were forced to leave in silence. But Aruna couldn't stop asking questions to Venga regarding what was said by Asobha in her presence. However, he evaded all her questions citing her insanity. On the next day, when Asobha was found dead, the will came as her ghost to haunt Venga. He couldn't bear that the property was slipping away from his hands just because of one paper which was left behind by a lady who could not even write or read properly. He tried to talk the lawyer into killing the will. But he was told back that Vaidhe was already aware of the will and she was coming to get the property transferred. Upon hearing that news, he feared to make any stupid moves as he was kept in the dark about what Vaidhe knew and didn't.

ꕥ

After Rama's death, Venga had heard about Vaidhe in one of the village gossips for the first time. He came to know that she was traumatised to death after hearing the news of Rama's demise. She was rushed to the hospital where she spent her days, missing all the final rites of Rama. After coming to her senses, she went wild and she was admitted to a mental asylum where she spent a few more days. When she was finally let go, she ran away from home. Rumour was that she had turned into a vagabond and was found at several places by several people. Venga was not aware that she had returned for his bad.

Vaidhe, after spending a considerable number of days as a vagabond, visited and settled at the mutt of Kaivar. It was only there that she could effortlessly calm herself. The saints at the mutt drew her with their mere conduct. After calming herself, she contacted her parents and put their worries about her to rest. Jana and Suneena too thought that sainthood was best for her daughter after the double tragedies she bore. After acquainting with her, the mutt asked her to go and look after their branch in Bani as Ajjamma had succumbed to her age. She hesitated at first but committed later. She posted a letter to her parents that she would visit them on her way to the mutt in Bani, but she arrived home along with the letter. She visited Bani mutt a few days after Asobha's death, and she had taken over the charge as its mother. That was when Byrappa informed the whereabouts of Vaidhe to the lawyer, and that is when the lawyer read the will to Vaidhe. She transferred all the possessions of Asobha to her name, and except for the five acres of red soil fields, she re-transferred everything else to Aruna. She donated the five acres to the mutt. It was her first step in making the mutt self-sustaining. She grouped up several women from the village and planted trees all around the borders. She planted trees for wood, fruit and shade. She carried on with seasonal farming in the remaining land. She made sure the mutt grew enough grain and vegetables for its own. Any donations she obtained from the people went into expanding the reach of the teachings of the Saint of Kaivar. With gracious donations coming in, she built a *bhajan* room within a year and a small school within two years. The prayers of the sage of Kaivar were heard every day and night by the disciples. Handpicked children were taught at the school – with limited resources at her disposal, she could only choose those who were very much in need of help. She roamed around the places, spreading the exuberance of life. The stories of her husband, from the mutt of Kaivar to its monastery in Bani, along with his teachings about farming, were not entirely lost on her. She recalled her words to Rama when she was lost in the tales of his travels, "I wish I had lived your life at least for a day." Rama was living in every act of hers, every day and every moment.

In a few years, Aruna visited the school of Kaivar mutt with her son. Vaidhe received her with such a smile that she herself never had on her face. The hospitality displayed by Vaidhe brought tears to Aruna's eyes. After Asobha's death, it did not take long for her to unearth the enigma in the words of her dying mother-in-law. However deep she pitied Vaidhe and how much ever she despised her husband, she did not reveal her mind to anyone for the same reason Asobha carried it to her grave. Standing in front of Vaidhe, receiving her hospitality with such a pristine smile, Aruna's heart longed to spit the truth out. "I have something to say about your husband," she said to Vaidhe. "Leave the dead to rest," Vaidhe replied with a smile and took Aruna around to show her the school.

Aruna started walking with Vaidhe but she was still confused. '*Should I tell her, or should I let it go? How can I let it go? Perhaps, the truth may add more bitterness to her grave past. However, the killer is a close reality in my life.*' Her confusion turned into fear in just a matter of seconds. Her sight turned to the caster plant on her path. As if someone planted a thought in her mind, she plucked a bunch of dried castor seeds and tied them in her saree drape. She walked with Vaidhe, smiling.

THE END

www.ingramcontent.com/pod-product-compliance
Lightning Source LLC
LaVergne TN
LVHW041218150826
845673LV00001B/445